C000077641

In Kinder's Mists

Pat Cunningham

Pat Cunningham

Pecsaeton Publishing

Published by
Pecsaeton Publishing

Flat 13, Clare House, Lime Avenue,
Derby, DE1 1TU, England
patrick@pecsaeton.co.uk
www.pecsaeton.co.uk

ISBN 978-0-9556325-0-1

© **Pat Cunningham 2007**

First published July 2007

The rights of Pat Cunningham as author of this work have been asserted by him in accordance with the Copyrights, Design and Patents Act, 1993

All rights reserved. No part of this publication may be reproduced, stored in a retrieval system or transmitted in any form or by any means, electronic, mechanical, photocopying, recording or otherwise without the prior permission Pat Cunningham.

British Library Cataloguing in Publication Data: a catalogue record for this book is available from the British Library.

Printed by Ta Kung Printing, Shenzhen, China

Front Cover: aircraft wreckage on a misty Kinder

'Well, with map-reading skills like yours you really need a GPS.'
Wies White, gift-giving, Christmas Eve 2001

Other books by the author:

Peakland Air Crashes: The North
Peakland Air Crashes: The Central Area
Peakland Air Crashes: The South
Published by Landmark Publishing, Ashbourne

Reactions to the Air Crashes series:

Excellent books, certainly far better than any others of the genre
Clive Teale, Nottingham, hill walker and private pilot

This series aims to set a benchmark. It is unlikely ever to be bettered
Julie Bunting, *Peakland Advertiser*

The three books make an excellent set
Malcolm Barrass, Air Historian, *Air of Authority* website.

Your excellent series of superb books
Alan Jones, Stalybridge, artist and aviation archaeologist

I find *The North* excellent too
John Ownsworth, Penistone, aviation archaeologist

I've enjoyed reading *The North*, as I did the last volume
Ian Howe, proofreader, for Landmark Publishing

In preparation:
Peakland Operational Aircrew, series
The Ignorant Walker's Companion

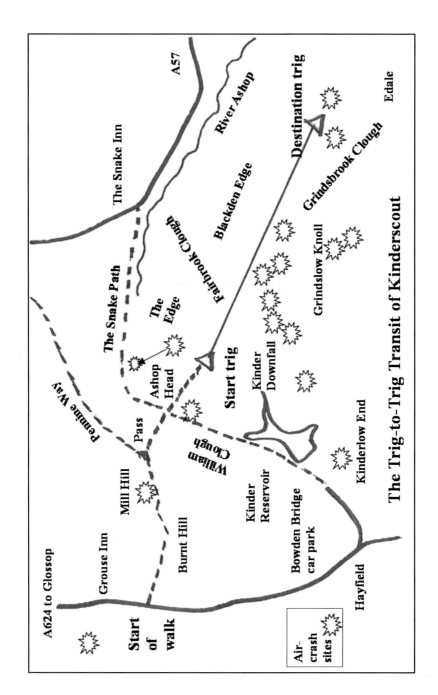

The Trig-to-Trig Transit of Kinderscout

Chapter One

Stunned by the implications of the call I let the phone settle onto its rest and looked unseeingly through the Christmas cards to the ranked books with their multi-coloured spines. Lucky unfeeling spines! For the shiver sent down mine by the call just ended had chilled me to the bone.

What I needed now was Helen's sound, stabilising calm. Above all, I needed the warmth of her presence. I knew I was not yet capable of rationally assessing the full ramifications of the call. Of accepting that past and present and life and death were indeed merely indivisible parts of an unceasing progression; that there was no free choice, only predetermined courses of action.

But Helen would help me with that. The snag being that in less than twelve hours she would be back with me. And before that I had to work out the least hurtful way of revealing to her that I had not only kept secret my brush with death on Kinder, just three months earlier, but all the nightmare awakenings of the past two years.

The call had left me torn between unwillingness and inability to take in what it had revealed. It had, quite literally, taken the ground out from under me. Yet as a flyer I knew how important it was to keep one's head out of the clouds and one's feet anchored firmly to the ground.

At the same time, although its revelations had rocked me to my foundations, I doubted that Helen would be in the least bit taken aback. But then her clear-sightedness has never failed to surprise me. Not least by apprehending how my return to flying would affect me. After all, for weeks beforehand I had been simply bubbling over in anticipation of that first refresher-training trip. And understandably so, for it had marked the end of the two most traumatic years in my life.

Flying to me had always been more of a vocation than a job. Yet although the accident inquiry had not only cleared me of blame for my crash but actually praised me, and my company had been unwavering in its support, the re-instatement of my medical licence had hung in doubt for interminable months. The first training flight had marked the end to all that. It had also coincided with what I knew to be one of the busiest days on Helen's client list. Yet when I had returned home in mid-morning, jaded and despondent, she had been waiting for me in my flat.

'Don't tell me, Mark.' Her embrace had been especially warm. 'The moment you got into that aeroplane you found things crowding in on you.'

'Yet I didn't have a qualm during the flight-simulator sessions.'

'But once you were actually airborne again you felt over-burdened.'

'Overburdened? With no passengers? And no crew? Just a fellow training captain?'

'Overburdened with baggage from the past.'

She had been right, of course. So that even before engine start my back hairs had lifted beneath the voiceless demand of those fourteen outraged souls, 'What moral right have you?'

And once airborne it had been even worse.

It stands to reason that in aviation, as in all aspects of life, crap sometimes happens. And then has to be lived with. Only everything I had ever lived for, together with all the physical and psychological rehabilitation of the last two years, had been thrown back into the balance by these utterly unlooked-for manifestations of my guilt.

'Great trip, Mark!' my colleague had grinned as we had walked back to the flight office after landing, 'We'll have you back earning your bread within the week.'

Only I had known differently. Conflicting emotions had warred within me throughout the flight. Not that there had been any real contest. I was simply too professional to risk saddling dependent passengers and crew with an emotionally unfit captain.

Yet what had come as the biggest shock of all was to have been so effectively ambushed by what Helen always calls my demons – though shunning jargon how she loves the graphic label! But then there had been so many examples of Helen's perceptive powers that I had long since learnt to find refuge where it offered; most often in the depths of my mind. Not that I had ever allowed myself to become complacent over the limited success I had achieved in concealing things from her. Indeed I loathed the circumstances that made it necessary.

'I'm like a counsellor,' Helen had maintained from the start, 'with just a tad of sports-injury experience thrown in.'

In fact, as a former county-class athlete she had far more than just a tad of trauma expertise. And for counsellor, read doctorate in clinical psychology with an international reputation and a busy consultant practice. Certainly, within an hour of our chance meeting on Kinder eighteen months before she had penetrated layers of my defences never so much as suspected by the Civil Aviation therapists.

'Mr Mark Johnston,' she had decided equably, 'you're holding back on me.' And then, glancing aside at my profile, 'Now why is that?'

This had by no means stopped her delving. So that even before we had descended half way down William Clough she had identified the nature of the guilt that rode me. More significantly she had led me to declare my conviction that nothing could relieve me of that guilt. A conviction she had vigorously set herself to oppose. Skilful though she had proved to be, however, I had managed to keep my core defences intact. Accordingly, long minutes after replacing the phone, I still shied from accepting that such a relief from guilt might now have been granted. Indeed I hardly dared entertain the notion. For even the possibility would overset my most steadfast beliefs. While the reality would overset credibility itself.

For a true evaluation, therefore, I really did need Helen. Only Christmas Eve notwithstanding she was presently winging her way back from a lecture commitment in the States. Meanwhile I disregarded both the fine tawny port decanted at my elbow and the seasonal mince pies she had baked for me. Instead I forced my thoughts to re-run that trans-Kinderscout walk I had made, just three months back. A walk that had clearly been of more significance than I dared believe even now.

Certainly until I saw Helen again I would shelve the question of why I had chosen that particular route. For tonight's bombshell revelation notwithstanding I still wanted to believe that I had selected the Kinder transit of my own free will. A moment's thought, of course, would have told me that it simply bristled with aviation associations; although other Peakland routes could have matched it on that score. But few upland tracts of Derbyshire are so devoid of distracting scenery. Indeed the virtually-featureless Kinderscout Plateau had proven itself eminently suited to the purpose of clearing the mind. Until my footing had given way and brought my head into contact with that rock ...

Chapter Two

Upon shouldering my rucksack on the day following that disastrous refresher-training flight I had pragmatically shelved the problem of my career. What I had set out to resolve instead had been the future of my relationship with Helen. For as one consequence of that all-too revealing flight it had become clear that I must at least reconsider my stance of holding back from her. Adopting that stance had already taxed me to the limit; to maintain it once Helen had dissected my reactions to the flight would be virtually impossible.

Clearly I had lost the career I loved. Equally clearly, in leaving Helen to discover for herself just how much of my trust I had withheld, I risked losing the woman I loved too. Accordingly my aim that day on Kinder had been to solve the dilemma this had posed. For to commit to a fuller relationship would mean admitting to the existence of a recurrent dream that was far too close to reality to disparage as a mere nightmare.

Ethically driven as she was, Helen had never sought to do anything but supplement the activities of the Ministry's medicos. Except that by the time she had come on the scene they had effectively given up on me, contenting themselves with making notes and muttering about post-traumatic stress disorder. Ethics too, had led to Helen refusing to formally enrol me as one of her patients, a professional stance I had last taxed her with only days before, choosing to put my own gloss on it, of course.

'It's because from the start you had designs on my body. So if you'd taken money they'd have defrocked you, or whatever they do to clinical psychologists.'

Her attire, or lack of it, at that moment, had made us both grin. Helen, the hussy, with not a trace of shame. In answer she had lifted to her feet and taken a step or two across the room, parodying my former halting gait and stiff arm.

'Your body was no great catch, Captain Mark, m'lad.' She had closed with me once more, advancing a finger. First she had touched it to my right arm, then, bending forwards, had run it lingeringly up the inside of my left thigh. 'You know your lesson.'

'Yes, Doctor Helen. Healer, Time, the Great, is.'

'You know very well I'd never say anything as crass.'

'No, you'd wrap it up so that it was both arcane and politically-correct.'

She had bridled at once. There were few things in which she was predictable. But in the same way that she shunned using professional jargon to patients, so she loathed platitudes. Just the same, she refused to be drawn further.

'The arm. The leg. Now they work.' Gravely she had spelled it out like the oft-told text it had become. 'And that's your proof that duty's price has been paid.' She had straightened slightly. 'But pragmatic as you are, even you can appreciate something tangible, like limbs that suddenly work again.' The same finger had tapped my temple. 'So just accept my word that relief from this perceived guilt of yours really will be furnished in its own good time.'

Only here even Helen had failed to convince. For neither she, nor anyone else, could tell me where such relief was to come from. More particularly as a Catholic upbringing still made it difficult for me to admit that I had long since lost all faith in religion, and therefore, in anything pertaining to the supernatural, to the spirit world, or to life after death.

'If there's anything in all that after-life stuff,' I had demanded of her months before, 'how is that so many people – and people dearly loved at that –, "pass beyond" without even fleetingly returning to give some solace to those left mourning them?'

'Theologians,' she had returned levelly, 'might argue that that's a rather naïve philosophy.'

And well they might. But it had been sound enough for me, forming the basis of my conviction that I could look to neither the living nor the dead to relieve me of my guilt. Not even to the unquiet souls who had nightly accused me of their deaths and had now, so disastrously, begun doing so in the air. And if not to them – my own dead –, then to whom, for pity's sake?

Yet, setting aside my now-fundamental disbelief in an afterlife and any form of spirit world, that early upbringing has left in its train a conscience that enjoys nothing better than facing me with moral issues. A conscience which now demanded to know whether my holding back from Helen was truly rooted in trauma, or in fear of once more embarking upon a committed relationship. It dared me, in particular, to deny the fact that in the general run of life my tendency is to take the easy path, regarding the familiar as safe and good, the unfamiliar as potentially both unsafe and bad.

As things were, life in general had become good. Indeed, thanks to Helen, life could not be better. But Helen had her own past, and doleful marriage to a philandering drunk behind her. Which meant that if I was wrong it was only too likely that I would turn the happiness of the present into a state of tethered misery for her. I had done grievous harm to so many of those who had placed their trust in me. To a former partner who, despite her repeated betrayal of every wedding vow, should still have been able to count on my support. More recently to so many of my hapless passengers, and members of my crew. How then, in the face of such cautionary examples, could I risk visiting disaster upon blameless Helen?

Chapter Three

To even approach accuracy, of course, any mulling over of my trans-Kinder walk should be reassessed in the light of tonight's phone call. But all I can usefully do at present is try to recreate the mindset that was driving me that day. For the only way to minimise the pain I cannot avoid causing Helen is to show her that in withholding my trust I have been acting under compulsion and not choice.

In the light of a mindset I must now see as naïve at best, I have to accept it as just one more of the imponderables of that walk that I had never given a thought to either local aviation activity or local air tragedies, not even as I had watched the Glossop bus speed off past the Grouse Inn. Yet I had often seen joyriding helicopters operating from the pub. And as I had negotiated the stile for Burnt Hill there had been no sense of shock as it come back to me that an American fighter pilot, lost and in thick cloud, had nosed his Mustang into the ground nearby.

It is also conceivable, of course, that unconscious reflections of that nature had already been disrupting my intended train of thought. Certainly, as I laboured up the slope, I remember making a determined effort to focus upon my relationship with Helen. But to the best of my knowledge the only distraction had been the relative lateness of the hour, for by then, thanks to various delays, it had been well on into the afternoon. Not that this had posed a problem, for I had still been left with ample time to do the walk then pick up the train from Edale, on the far side of Kinder, or failing that, find overnight accommodation.

Thanks largely to Helen's programme of rehabilitating walks my formerly traumatised arm and leg had weeks since regained their respective functions. Indeed, beyond a slight headcold, my physical state had given no qualms. The weather, on the other hand, had proved a sad disappointment.

'Low cloud and poor visibility particularly on the high ground,' the TV weather lady had promised, 'followed by heavy and persistent rain.'

Ideal conditions, in fact, for my envisaged compass walk. Except that the tops of the moorlands stretching away before me had been completely in the clear.

There had been rain-bearing clouds piling blackly to the east, for sure, yet the visibility had been limited only by the intervening terrain. But then I would not have dreamed of complaining about such a let-down. Leave it to the world of academe to treat the common-or-garden bloody obvious as something of great import. So yet again the met service had got it wrong. So what was new?

Nearing the Burnt Hill summit it had been time to pause for breath, when unzipping against a largely ruinous drystone wall had represented a double relief. The now barely-distinguishable traffic hum from the Hayfield-Glossop Road had been replaced by the soughing of a breeze across heather masses in which white flowers still predominated. Although enough of these had turned to wash the moors with at least a promise of the purple glory yet to come.

Clambering onto a stile I had found myself peering into the eyes of two startled-looking Derbyshire Gritstones, a ram who had glassily stared me out, and a ewe who on the instant had vented her bladder. I had called cheerily, 'Hello, sheep!' Only at this they had made off, looking back on occasion with something of a shifty air, their hooves crunching over the dry, burnt-off fronds of heather.

'Heather soon gets too tough for grouse and hares,' a hill-farmer had told me, 'give it a few years and even sheep can't handle it. So whenever the weather's suitable, we burn it off.'

Indeed I had been able to make out smoke smudges where heather burning was actually being carried out on Chunal Moor, and by the look of it, on Kinder itself. And I had imagined that, like the region's gardeners, the rangers, shepherds, or estate workers engaged in the task would also welcome rain. In their case, let the underlying peat catch fire and the moor could burn for months!

At which point my concentration had been further diverted by a now-familiar nagging at my subconscious. Having plagued me for some while it had grown even more persistent in the last few days, only to remain, infuriatingly, just beyond recall. Something to do with a colour combination. Red, I fancied, and blue. So that I remember balancing on the stile, craning my head after the by-then distantly browsing pair. Except that neither suspiciously unshorn back had displayed any trace of colour; long fleeces and lack of ownership marks almost certainly branding them as illegal immigrants from another moor, busily contributing to overgrazing.

I had now come to the pull up Mill Hill, until relatively recently a quagmire but paved since with Yorkshire-stone slabs, most reclaimed from the floors of Blake's dark satanic mills. Mossy tints are already hastening their adoption by the moors, although many bear traces of their former use. Recognising the necessity for such paving, but regretting its unyielding surface, I had moved morosely over threaded bolts, shaft holes, and splashes of colour from paints and glutinous spillages. My pole ends had poked at a splodge of purple, a run of yellow; at a red spot, and then a splash of blue. Red ... and blue. And again that recurrent, subliminal niggle had nagged at me. And again, infuriatingly, had simply refused to surface.

A sudden murmur had dispelled the irritation on that occasion, drawing my eye high and to the right as a Manchester-bound airliner had materialised from one of the ragged fringes of cloud now moving in. For once the sight had brought me no pleasure, conjuring up, as it had, all my doubts from the previous day. I had been tired, of course, because predictably enough the nightmare had re-visited in its full intensity. After which, trying to reconcile doubts and duty had robbed me of many more hours of sleep.

The crew of that airliner, I had reflected, had been kept clear of Kinder's rocks by their electronics. But stark evidence that it had not always been so had awaited me just a few yards further on, where the path bent around a peat gully.

The gully was unusually green and grassy-floored for the area, with washes of sand and gritstone debris brought down by the rains. Only there was other debris, spitefully white, but in places silvered with pitted chrome. There were wing sections, and engines whose gaping cylinders revealed connecting rods which had last driven pistons over sixty years before. The impact point was a little higher, still bare of vegetation but with more wreckage. And everywhere there were metal gobs, white and brittle, or hard like frozen tears.

Scanning the terrain, with Mill Hill rising only a few feet more, it became yet again a case of, how near! and yet how far! And as I did whenever I passed that way I had duly wondered at the vagaries of chance, and crossed my fingers in a, 'There, but for the grace of God', gesture.

I had found too, somewhat to my surprise, that I was still able to regard the scene dispassionately. Although my ability to do so in the face of my own crash had set me to reasoning. I had concluded, however, that whereas this was one of so many local crashes caused by a fatally flawed decision, my decision, though fatal, had certainly not been flawed.

It had been a point made much of by both the investigating board and the medics, each in their own way intent on rooting out what they regarded as my too stubborn retention of guilt.

'But should the same situation obtain in the future, Captain Johnston,' the president of the board had coaxed, 'would you give the same order?'

'I would, sir,' I had replied.

And to a man the other members of the board had nodded approval.

But that, of course, had been to view the matter from a clinically-professional standpoint. A standpoint that neither guilt nor nightmares took notice of. Easily enough done, just the same, in waking hours. So much so, indeed, that viewing the Mill Hill wreckage on that occasion I had been able to do so, not just dispassionately, but with a jaundiced eye.

For some impressionable passer-by, undoubtedly regarding air crashes as romantic – and certainly oozing with what they would have believed to be empathy – had gathered stones to form a memorial cross. Only nobody had died here. For after the ferry pilot had ignored a height warning from his colleague and bellied into the ground in cloud, both men had walked away. Indeed the only thing worthy of remembrance here is Captain Lamplugh's celebrated quote opining that the air is 'terribly unforgiving of any carelessness, incapacity or neglect.'

Chapter Four

Viewed from the summit of Mill Hill the weather-sculpted rocky outcrops of The Edge, the northern rim of the Kinder Plateau, undulate away towards Fairbrook Naze. To the right the eye is taken by the crag-faced ridge sweeping around to Kinderlow End, two-and-a-half miles distant. And on that occasion I had, as always, been duly impressed. For although lifting to just eleven hundred feet above its valleys, and standing at only a little over two thousand feet above sea level, the Kinder Plateau offers both grandeur and remoteness. Hardly surprising then that it became the focus of aspirations to walk freely at a time when landowners jealously guarded the moors against public access.

Certainly this would have been in my mind as I came to the pass where the Pennine Way crosses the Snake Path. For the pass's summit was chosen for the so-called victory meeting of the 1932 Mass Trespass of Kinder, a problematical foray which, although arguably setting back the walkers' cause for a good decade, has become the very stuff of romance. Indeed the pass itself is viewed as romantic by air-crash anoraks because a helicopter lifting footpath material tumbled benignly to its destruction just a few yards off.

Mass protests and overloaded helicopters aside, I can personally vouch for the fact that true romance really has flowered in the vicinity of the pass. For just six months after my crash I had been endeavouring to force my gimpy limbs to obey me as I cast a loop around the Kinder Downfall from Bowden Bridge car park. My aim had been to ascend William Clough, view the Downfall, then carry on to return by way of Kinderlow End.

It had been some considerable time since I had climbed the increasingly popular stepped path from the pass to the top of

Ashop Head. More recently my liking for solitude had seen me angling off from the pass and up the rough ground to gain the less frequented northern rim path along The Edge, only then to take my first rest, and have a snack.

On that first High Peak outing after my crash, however, Fortune had determined that I should mount the steps instead. Having reached the top, therefore, I had sheltered from the near-gale behind the cairn, completed my break, and had been re-packing my rucksack when another walker, looping the Downfall in the opposite direction, as it transpired, had paused prior to embarking upon the descent to the pass. It had been Helen.

She periodically employs that first encounter to charge that my holding back from her is an inbuilt characteristic.

'You're evading the issue, Mark,' she had chided only days since. 'But then you did that from the start. "People'd pay to see the Downfall in this wind", indeed!'

'And so they would have.'

For when the Downfall's waters are blown skywards and backwards to shower sheep and walkers for eighty yards and more upstream it is a truly spectacular sight. Indeed there had been an occasion when, seeing the smoke-white plume from a distance, I had taken it for a heather burn.

'But giving me to understand that you too were on your way down?'

'I didn't actually say which way I was going. It's what you assumed. But then there were the vibes! They seduced me – just that once, you understand –, into bending the truth. Besides, in the rough bits you were glad enough of my arm.'

'You, recognise vibes! And your arm!' She had snorted. 'The record slow-descent of William Clough, and me as your crutch.'

However, it had been another exchange from our first meeting which had come back to me as I had scaled the steps to position for the mind-clearing 'trig-to-trig' jaunt. Helen had referred to a local legend.

'You know,' she had confided, smiling, 'I've never been up on Kinder before, yet just back there, above Mermaid's Pool, I was overtaken by déjà vu. The Mermaid's spirit, would you say?'

I had already resolved to keep this woman from slipping away, deciding in that first instant to turn in my tracks and descend again. But while fearing to antagonise her I had felt obliged to take a stand against even fringe supernaturalism.

'Being a time-served pragmatist, never! Besides, she doesn't wander, they say. Simply takes midnight skinny-dips on Easter-Eve.'

And we had laughed. But I had uncharacteristically found myself paying respect even to feyness; as a notion embraced by Helen, at least. And conceding more readily, that the susceptible might well find themselves ensnared by the tricks and mind games played by these upland moors.

Indeed unknown to Helen evidence of one moorland ensnarement had been only yards distant. A pile of duralumin, just beyond the top cairn, greyly forlorn within a shallow gully, but once sprayed duck-egg blue. Merely the start, in fact, of the mile-long debris trail of two formating jets which, caught below cloud, had zoomed up from the level of the Kinder Reservoir, collided, then skimmed on, intertwined and disintegrating, before plunging into the depths of Black Ashop Moor. Their whereabouts had remained a mystery until some days later when a walker, heading along The Edge from Ashop Head, had come upon the body of one of the pilots. At the very spot, as it happened, where having angled up to reach The Edge, I had subsequently become accustomed – and purely by chance, I maintain – to taking that first break!

Chapter Five

On the crowd-avoiding trans-Kinder jaunt the starting point for my straight-line trek is Kinder's westerly trig point. The destination is another trig point something over three miles to the east. These four-sided, four-foot-high, concrete columns were sited on their prominences by the mapmakers of the Ordnance Survey in the years spanning the Second World War. Designed to provide the base points for the trigonometrical framework of the maps, they were initially regarded as garish intrusions into the landscape. Over the years, however, they became cherished, so that, on being made redundant by satellites, many were adopted by folk who undertook to periodically re-paint them.

An undertaking 'more honour'd in the breach than in the observance', as Helen once had it, such quotes being, in my experience, her sole pandering to the first she took at Girton before passing on to gain higher distinctions still. But then for distinctions Kinder's westerly trig too is pre-eminent among its kind, for isolated on its rocky base it stands aloof above the original, long-since tumbled column in a moorland buy one, get one free.

In view of the forecast weather I had anticipated forging off into the fog to reach it, knowing from previous treks that, even in good weather, the undulating terrain would hide the column until I was quite close. Having measured the direction on the map, 122 degrees, or south-eastish, it had taken just moments to set up the compass. First off, 122 on the ring, then rotate the old torso until the wobbling, north-seeking red needle matches up with the broad North arrow. Then look up. And out there in the *bundu*, but directly ahead, has to be the yet-hidden trig column.

Before striding off, however, I had dwelled a few more moments. Supplementary these, but the fruit of hard-won experience. And of vital importance to any bold walker with serious aspirations to become an old walker.

First, a glance to ascertain that Ashop Head really was behind me still, that nobody had moved it. Then a second check, to confirm that what I had aligned with the broad North arrow was indeed the wobbling red needle and not its tail, coloured white on my Silva compass. For had I inadvertently lined up the tail, that would have had me tramping off in the reverse direction – in navigators' terms, the reciprocal direction –, back towards Ashop Head.

This common-sense double check was the walker-navigator's equivalent of the woodworker's maxim of 'measure twice, cut once'. In similar vein I had drilled out the plastic base-plate of the compass to take a stouter securing cord than Silva's had deemed necessary. And I remember now, with no little degree of irony, just how smugly proud I had been to have improved upon Mssrs Silva's time-tested design. In the same breath I had even congratulated myself on having saved a few pounds by investing in the cheapest of their range, the model 'suitable for schools, scouts, beginners'. How, indeed, do the mighty set themselves up!

But, well satisfied with my preparations at the time, I had then selected a heather tussock as a marker. Had the mist really been down such a track-guide might have had to be just feet off, calling for frequent compass checks to ensure that I was holding my correct heading. As it was, with virtually unlimited visibility, more distant markers had sufficed. A half a mile to go. Which, taking into account the pathless terrain before me, I would have expected to take some fifteen minutes.

Off the path the ground had at once become more broken, the heather carpet being scored by peat channels which had deepened as I had progressed, until the trig column had come gratifyingly into view almost directly on my nose. Gratifyingly, for the compass is a demanding slave. For a start, be just one degree off track and after travelling sixty miles you will be a whole mile astray. And straying off heading is just one of an extended family of compass errors. But for me, the trig column was exactly where it should have been, and I was content.

Re-setting the course for the distant destination trig was again a matter of moments. But where judging distance gone is concerned I am no great shakes. Counting the number of paces on a knotted cord overtaxes my concentration at the best of times. I am more of a time man, and on flat, unobstructed ground I walk at about three miles an hour. But Kinder is neither flat nor unobstructed. Besides, I take rests, tiddling or tippling whenever I feel the need. So, averaging my previous times, I would have known to look for the target trig after something like two hours and twenty minutes.

The critical thing would have been the compass heading. And that I would have paid strict attention to, my long-term career goals being retirement and a fat pension. The mantra so beloved of the early jet-jockeys, 'Kick the tyres, light the fires, and last one to forty-thousand feet's a sissy', had never been mine, although many others had paid the price of such cavalier inattention to detail.

So that just a mile off my right shoulder, beside the path at Cluther Rocks, were the remains of a strayed Hampden bomber whose crew had taken insufficient care in calculating a revised heading for their base. And just beyond that a light-aeroplane pilot, flying in patchy cloud, had been unaware that an exceptionally strong tailwind was speeding him past his intended destination and into Kinderlow End. A plaintive echo of Lewis Carroll. Alice's, 'Are we nearly there?' and the Queen's, 'Nearly there! Why, we passed it ten minutes ago'.

Such moorland tragedies have been the subject of various books and websites written, in the main, by air-crash enthusiasts. Most adopt a regrettably melodramatic style, flirt with 'mystery' causes, and even introduce ghosts; all three being sure pointers to non-aviator authorship. For aviators know that aeroplanes do not mysteriously fly into hills and kill their gallant crews. Although many a crew member has killed the gallant machine that has done nothing but obey the hand-mind combination directing it.

Nor does a crash automatically turn even wartime aircrews into heroes, the vast majority of Peakland accidents having been caused by very human failings. As for the dramatic tension embroidered by such enthusiast scribes, the kindly truth is that few airmen who fatally crashed in the area even remotely suspected that cloud-shrouded death was but an instant away.

But that flyers and non-flyers should have different standpoints is not surprising. For as a truism from flying's earliest days has it, 'To build an aeroplane is something, to fly it is everything!' The lamentable reality being that few who love aviation can aspire to fly in their own right.

High time, I would have resolved at that juncture, to finally set about my task. After all, I had specifically chosen Kinder for its lack of distracting features, the central plateau offering bland moorland in abundance, but little else of scenic value.

This is not to say that Kinder lacks an intrinsic beauty, although only from the air can it be seen as a many-channelled delta. Yet even the walker can marvel at the way the various flows combine to carve out such precipitous gulches as Fair Brook, Blackden, Crowden, Grindsbrook, and the Kinder Downfall. Indeed Helen likens the plateau's drainage system to life itself, with each part exerting its effect upon some other, no matter how distant. Certainly, while edgily apprehensive in the face of a Christmas Eve changed unimaginably by the phone call, I have to concede that had the course of my life altered by even a jot I would not have met Helen, or known the happiness she has brought me since.

Although confident in my ability to hold a compass heading, I would still have been on guard against complacency. The lesson learnt too late by the pilot who had inadvertently flown north-east instead of north-west and left his Anson to litter the hillside barely a mile to my right. Complacency too, had killed the ill-disciplined – some might prefer, high-spirited – pupil-pilot who had deliberately deviated sixty miles from his assigned course and crashed in cloud only yards from the Anson. Being so far off course his Harvard trainer had not been located for six days.

Thought of which had turned my mind to another fatal crash which, had it happened in the Peak District, would have given the mystery-at-any-price votaries a field day. For when the private-pilot son of radio-Goon Michael Bentine went missing the authorities concluded that he had crashed into the sea. Bentine, however, a lifelong clairvoyant, 'saw' the machine in woodland. And a full month later it was duly found near Petersfield, nose-down in a clump of trees.

I had breasted on, peering in the direction of Crowden Tower. And I would have pondered anew upon the vagaries that are so often all that separate the quick and the dead. For when the pilot of a Blenheim had edged beneath the clouds and clipped the ground the aircraft had barely been damaged. Despite which none of the four occupants had survived.

For some time my straight-line track had obliged me to wade the marshy watershed. Then, as the plateau had curved and dipped, it had taken me clear of it. But from then on I had been committed to the physically-demanding negotiation of the ever-deepening water channels cutting across my line of travel. And it had been at this stage that I had begun to realise that such labour was taking far greater toll of my mental resources than I had allowed for.

Just as well then, that I had not set my mind to resolving the issue of my guilt feelings. For that is an area where Helen and I must remain at odds. Helen holds that my 'close pent-up guilts' will pass with time. For my part I cannot see how this can come about. For although the decision I made to get my aircraft stopped led to carnage, it was professionally correct. Consequently I had never doubted that the baleful disturbances to my nights were the business of my subconscious; to be ignored, therefore, at the intellectual level. But emerging so damningly during the training flight meant that they had now begun invading my conscious mind too. And rather than the lessening effect Helen has always looked to, that had represented a marked increase in my 'guilts'.

Helen frequently accuses me of wilfully clinging to my guilt. Generally, however, she takes the line that I am 'more sinned against than sinning' – she always allies herself with Shakespeare eventually. But this is a stage we have reached time and again. One I recognise, moreover, as being perilously fraught. And Helen knows this.

'So here we stick,' she will say, half-ruefully, half-resignedly. And on occasion not without some decidedly unprofessional exasperation. Recently she charged hotly, 'You puke at the notion of "big hugs". Well, Mr Johnston, watching you hug your precious guilt makes *me* puke. I'm real. Hug me.'

And so I had, of course. And in doing so had successfully defused that particular crisis too. For she comes so very close to calling it as it is. Despite having not the slightest inkling of the dream.

Chapter Six

Each gully had now yawned up to twenty feet deep, steeply sided with the dark-brown to jet-black peat the Irish once called turf. In fact the Kinder Plateau transit is largely a matter of struggling with such gullies. Breathlessly so given a headcold. And on that occasion mine had so developed that swallowing had not even produced a wheeze from my ears, let alone a clearing click. And I remember the relief – shameful, but undeniable – that had swept me once it had struck home that unless my ears cleared in a day or so I would have a legitimate excuse to call off my next refresher flight: in aviation one never takes a chance with bunged up ears, the penalty being excruciating pain and every chance of permanently damaged hearing!

The slate-grey stones capping Fairbrook Naze, to my left, had marked off the first mile. By which time the steadily lowering clouds had begun spotting me with rain and the breeze had turned decidedly chilly. As always, however, a marked lessening of the wind chill could be found in the water channels, the deepest of which were locally termed 'cloughs', the minor ones I was battling with 'groughs', and their heather-upholstered rims 'hags'.

So, hags and groughs! Smacking of Billy-Goat Gruffs, of rickety-rackety bridges, of witches, and of trolls. And to the over-imaginative the Kinder plateau, so late on an Autumn day, with the clouds sullen and the stiffening breeze whining through rush and cotton grass, would have made a fitting setting for such bogeys.

Indeed on that late afternoon it had been a scene truly suggestive of utter desolation, with all contrast low, and any colour drear, a bleak, seemingly-unending panorama of featureless dun-hued mounds and forlorn troughs. To all intents and purposes it had been quite devoid of life. Yet as I had breasted up onto a hag, a mountain hare, startled by my sudden appearance, had looked, twitched, leapt high, then loped away. It had yet to don its winter whites, being coated still in its summer brown. Or perhaps awareness of global warming was more universal that one might have thought.

Time had been passing, however, so I had pressed on. Only to become conscious once again of that only-too-niggling combination of blue and red that had first begun to irk me a fortnight before on the Lathkill, near Cales Dale. Sheep had been grazing among the rock-strewn trees, those nearby scampering upslope at my approach, the youngsters butting at their mothers' udders so strenuously as to lift those matrons off their feet. Then, as I had idly taken in the red and blue ownership splotches on their fleeces, it had been as if something long dormant in my mind had stirred. To date, however, whatever it was had stubbornly refused to emerge.

Now, fairly committed on Kinder, I had realised that the subliminal nagging was actually becoming insistent, as if setting foot on the plateau had brought about some significant change. Nothing had surfaced for all that, however, and again I had put it out of mind. After which it had been back to the drear onward plod, head down, eyeing every footfall, easing both ascent and descent with my trusty hiking poles. Mere, morass, and marsh; mud, mire, and muck. Exactly as before.

Certainly there had been little enough to see. To the left, both Fairbrook Clough and the weather-modelled, Muppet-like rocks of Seal Edge sat well below my horizon. To the right was an apparently-unnoteworthy mound of hag, grough, and piled boulders. Just the same it held the remains of both a Dragon Rapide biplane airliner and another RAF Anson, this one crewed entirely by Poles. In these two incidents nobody had died. Yet when a Wellington bomber had been blindly descended into Upper Tor – just a few minutes further along my route – only the rear gunner had survived, his turret having broken away to bowl off downhill and safely deposit him far below in Grindsbrook Clough.

All at once, I recall, I had been swept by rain flurries. And it had suddenly struck me that dusk was on its way. Not that this had been of undue concern, for I had a head-mounted torch that would be more than sufficient to light my way. And to see off bogeys.

'Ee-up, youth,' the suddenly-uncertain hag would croak, 'I don't care for yon one-eyed chap.'

'Not flashing like that, m'duck,' her troll consort would quaver. 'Let's mek oursen scarce.'

The whimsy that bogey-folk might indeed frequent these upland moors is, admittedly, made rather easier to entertain under the darkening effect of lowering cloud; only someone entirely lacking imagination could fail to concede that. Indeed in such conditions even the vacuous notion that ghostly airmen might linger on the plateau might seem at least momentarily tenable, especially as the psyche predisposes the most pragmatic of us to a good ghost story.

Just the same I still wonder that a sensationalist website devoted to sightings of spectral aircraft on Kinder can draw so many appreciative 'hits'. Or that dilettante mystics can dub placid Longdendale, not that far distant, 'The Haunted Valley'. For my part I subscribe to the view of a veteran habitué of the district, a veteran Peak Park Ranger and Mountain Rescue Service volunteer.

'These moors,' he declares, 'have their own mystique, but not a single mystery.'

Only neither soundly-based opinions nor contemporary records cut much ice with conspiracy theorists and ghost mongers. Personally, I have no truck with the breed.

Helen, of course, had taken me to task on that head.

'You're so sceptical! Can't you concede that there just might be a case for there being "more things in heaven and earth", darling?'

But here I had been on my own ground.

'Virtually all aircraft crashes are caused by their crews. So ghost aviators wouldn't leap out going "Boo!" They'd skulk, too conscience stricken to show their faces. No, all ghost mongers are cranks.'

She had regarded me reprovingly. 'Maybe just the tiniest touch of "the price of everything, and the value of nothing" would you say?'

'Quote him until the cows come home, but Shakespeare knew nothing about flying.'

'No more did Oscar Wilde, Captain Mark Johnston, sir. But he knew a lot about sceptics. And cranks. And cynics.'

I had been traversing an area of springy turf, of very nearly lawn quality, with a fringing smother of bilberry. And there had been the occasional swathe of pure white sand, lending just a little more credibility to the geologists' version of Kinder ghosts; that this whole upland plateau had once been a coastal estuary. As if!

Half way across the plateau, with the craggy tip of Grindslow Knoll just breaking the skyline to my right. In its time the Knoll had stopped the downward plunge of a Cessna, its two occupants making their own way down to the Nag's Head Inn in Edale. The night-flying crew of a Heyford biplane bomber, however, thirteen miles off course, had been nowhere near as fortunate, perishing in a fireball.

But already my attention had been drawn to my left, to where the distant, rain-blurred ridges of Alport Castle and the Derwent Edges formed a misty skyline over the Derwent Valley's dams. For that aviation truly has its mark on all this Peakland area, in an interweave of fact, fantasy, fiction, controversy, and wishful thinking, is made manifest in the wrangling over the extent to which the Derwent Dams were used by the celebrated Dambusters – Richard Todd's blokes. But then it is utterly in keeping with the persona of the area that any association with aviation should be shrouded as much in myth and mystery as in the High Peak's seasonal mists.

I had lengthened my stride, resolutely putting my best stick forward. 'Red, on blue …' Damn! The swinish thing was back with me yet again! Irritated, I had jabbed a stick into an inoffensive mound of peat. Then paused, held in mid stride, struck by the realisation that two weeks before, in Lathkill, when the pestering Red-on-Blue nuisance had first come to me, I had been using Helen's walking poles. And that she favoured one red pole, one blue! And there amidst Kinder's bogs I had yelled aloud. That plaguey irritant finally scratched! Nothing to do with sheep. Red stick, blue stick. And that was it.

Except that, at the next step, the niggle had surfaced yet again. On I had stamped, poles jabbing. Good try, Intellect! But not even a tiny bit good enough!

The faint, insistent buzzing of a light aeroplane pursuing its way up the Newlands Valley had distracted me.

'As long as you know what you're up to,' I had mouthed, hoping that in these rapidly deteriorating conditions the pilot was keeping an eye on the high ground closing in ahead of him. 'Pilot proceeded blindly through cloud' had been the gist of so many Peakland air-accident reports.

Yet more of Peakland's air-crash victims had believed themselves to be flying over a low-lying area when, in fact, they had been over the high moorlands. But then how surprising is that! For take the weather barometer out of granny's hall, change the caption from 'Fair, Windy, Wet, and Stormy' to 'Height Above Sea Level', and you have the aircraft altimeter. As with every device, the important thing is to know its quirks and limitations.

Back in the wartime days, before taking off from his near-sea-level airfield in Lincolnshire or Yorkshire, a pilot would set the altimeter needle to zero. All things being equal, this meant that when he arrived back over the airfield a reading of 2,000 feet would tell him that he had 2,000 feet of unobstructed air below him. On the other hand, had he wound up over the High Peak instead, then he would have been at exactly the same level as the Kinder Plateau!

Chapter Seven

The destination trig column had finally come into view, and exactly on line at that, proving that nothing but the magnetic north pole had been affecting my compass. Bleaklow, not that far off, was notorious for its weird magnetic properties. Not Kinder, however. But well worth checking for. Just in case some newly emergent subterranean lodestone should have begun pulling the needle astray. Some geopathic influence, perhaps; some ley lines coming into unfavourable conjunction; or some hill-spirit's malevolent spell. Peat shrinkage causing the regurgitation of some aeronautical debris might suffice; let alone of a whole machine, like the Lancaster bomber swallowed by similar black peat, near Ely. But nothing like that on Kinder. Although Kinder does boast a singular anomaly. For while the straight line drawn on the map between my two trig points cuts the path along the rim of Blackden Edge, the actual straight-line path on the ground never does so. An Ordnance Survey conspiracy, perhaps?

I had forgotten how habitually boggy the far stretch of Kinder was, and how full of rush-girdled pools between which even the firmest ground is a waste of russet-tipped cotton grass. Circumspection is always indicated on the moors but, momentarily distracted, I had tripped and fallen forwards, elbow-deep into a sodden, impact-cushioning bed of sphagnum moss. Also known as bog, or peat moss, the sphagnum variety flourishes in the upper moorlands, having ages past taken over from the trees. A food beloved by orchids, with a sex life not entirely devoid of interest, the ancients valued its healing properties and used it as a wound dressing. Interesting stuff. Although at that moment I merely cursed it. But undeniably interesting, just the same.

Approaching the trig column, I remember puffing a little. But that had been the effect of the headcold again, for the slope is hardly demanding. What would have been more in my mind was that, starting only two hundred yards beyond the column, was the wreckage trail of a Halifax, and not much further to the right, that of a Wellington. Both bombers had been many miles away from where they thought they were, and both had been descending, expecting to break cloud over their low-lying airfields. Only high-standing Kinder had broken them first. And with rain pattering freely on my face as I looked upwards into the overcast I had pictured unbroken layered cloud, just like this, extending downwards through many thousands of feet, its base draped wetly across this unfeeling upland. And I had pursed my lips in sympathy for the Canadians in the Halifax, and the Britons in the Wellington.

The weather, and unreliable weather forecasts, were almost invariably major factors in such tragedies. But then the prediction I had counted upon that very afternoon had shown how poorly-served even today's user can be. On the other hand what is the real risk of coming to grief on such moors as Kinderscout? And to a lone, but sensibly equipped venturer, in particular, even if caught in mid-plateau by a freezing fog.

Accept at once that Kinder is no Siberia. To the north and the south an unmistakable path is, at most, a thirty-minute stumble away; to east and west, a little longer. And while craggy edges abound, prominent paths give warning that the plateau's rim is close at hand. Little risk then. Always provided one keeps a level head. And does not give way to panic. Or even to fear of what the mist might hold.

Kinder's eastern trig pillar, like its westerly counterpart, has gum erosion, the exposed root standing a good two feet proud of the pond besieging it. Not being a bagger of prominent peaks, and seeing no point in wading, I had stayed on the firm ground some yards distant. The trig-to-trig exercise, for what it was worth, was well and truly over.

Only then had it struck me that although I had barely got started on my intended retrospective I had not simply made progress, but significant progress at that, presumably by some subconscious infusion of impressions. For I now knew that no matter how shaky my future in aviation might be, and how loudly my conscience might squawk about self interest, Helen was altogether too important to risk losing.

On the other hand I had made not the slightest progress in seeking out any strategy for freeing me from my guilt.

Dully, I had done a protracted turnabout in the welling peat, the surface of the pool writhing with interlacing ringlets as the downpour had intensified. It had been Sod's law with a vengeance that I now had exactly the weather I had envisaged for the compass exercise, a misty, rain-swept nothingness. But all too late.

In fact, I had noted, two hours and thirty-five minutes too late, for it had been that long since I had left the first trig. But now night was pressing. So which of the several paths to take down to Edale? I had turned, I remember, and had taken a step or two into the heather when a grouse had whirred explosively from beneath my feet. For the fraction of a second we had been nose to beak before, with a frantic spread of wings, it had powered away to one side with an alarm call so successful as to alarm the bejasus out of me.

But who could blame the grouse? Seeing that the moors would soon be closed for a day or two to allow the Sportsmen to slaughter its kind at will. Although who can say how things might change should the geneticists develop a strain of Kalashnikov-toting Sportsgrouse capable of shooting back? Just the same, there is no denying that the upland moors as we enjoy them today owe virtually everything to the rich man's lust for blood; even burning off the heather being, to a large extent, a measure to promote the breeding and well being – no matter how short-lived – of King Red Grouse.

No blame then, to the bird, but what the confrontation had told me was that negotiating the groughs had tired me rather more than I had realised. Had made me a little more pale and interesting … More pale, and it could be, more emotionally vulnerable …

Getting under way just moments later, it had been to realise that both the visibility and the light had lessened markedly. Not that this had been a problem, for any south-westish heading would take me to the edge path. And from there, even in the poorest light, I could not fail to pick out one of the well-defined tracks that lead down into Grindsbrook Clough, and Edale. It had been with no qualms about the route then, that I had set off once again.

I had reached a half-hearted count of just a hundred paces gone when the need to tell Helen what I had decided had overcome me. No matter how the decision had been made, I knew I had to let her know what it was. Accordingly, I had poised on the edge of a grough and flipped open the phone. Only to find that, having omitted to charge the battery for some days, the thing was utterly and uselessly dead! Nor did the reflection that the Hope Valley was largely a no-signal area anyway ease my irritation in the slightest.

Forging onwards, and just yards later, I had again tut-tutted in frustration, this time becoming conscious once more of that illusive niggle in my brain: red, on blue; blue, on red. And when I had such truly portentous issues to address, too! Yet how to ignore something that provoked notice, then tantalized from the very edge of recall?

Helen tells me that by stimulating a certain area of the brain a surgeon can induce an action replay of the past. But infuriating as a refractory notion may be, brain surgery might be a bit extreme.

I had grasped my walking poles more firmly. And I remember concluding, possibly rather too smugly, that although I had failed to solve the most major of my problems, nevertheless I had moved things on a very fair way.

Perhaps I had become a little careless; but if so I had been unaware of it, and looking back I can see myself swinging off in fine style, neither finding, nor expecting to find, an actual track going my way. For, despite the growing gloom, there had still been light enough to keep me clear of the deepest groughs and the messiest meres. Then, just as I had been about to negotiate a really serious-sided grough, a sheep had lurched to its feet – unexpectedly, but not as startlingly so as that grouse –, then lumbered off. I recollect, as I registered its going, that nagging thought interposing yet again, and as inconsequentially as ever, for this animal's fleece, like those of the pair on Mill Hill, was innocent of ownership marks. Yet still I remember improvising and idiotically bellowing out, 'Hoo, Ewe! – owned by who? Shepherd Red or Shepherd Blue?' And I fancy it was at that moment that the ground gave way beneath my heels.

I recall feeling that I was fortunate in still being some way short of the rim path. For although approaching Kinder's edges at dusk is not necessarily fraught, it pays to be alert. Here, as I had realised on the instant, nothing more threatening had happened than that a clump of heather forming the hag had broken off. Indeed, I had begun laughing as I had gone bum-borne downwards, my heels furrowing into the peat, my wrist-looped sticks, already set at full extension for the Edale descent, flailing at arms length.

I remember my right heel catching suddenly, and not releasing, and then the shooting pain that shot through my knee as my body pivoted around the trapped heel, so that in a further instant I was head down, and sliding on, but now with both feet free. I distinctly remember a double feeling of relief, first that I had got away with it, that the ankle had not fractured; and secondly that it was not the leg Helen had recently spent so much time over. I recollect that most distinctly ...

Chapter Eight

What I next remember, is the sound of water. But I could not understand why the light had faded so. Nor why I had been content to simply lie there since coming to my senses, as I knew I had, for what must have been a reckonable passage of time. No more could I fathom the uncomfortably-suffused pressure in my throat. And when I tried to sit up I found I was as powerless to do so as the waking Gulliver tied down by a myriad threads. Except that he was fictional. And although I found difficulty in relating to anything at that moment my head was threatening to split itself apart in such an attention-seeking way that I was nothing if not mortally real. Besides, in the last two years I had become an authority on differentiating between the dreaming and the waking states.

I tried to move my right hand. But found it would not budge. And I recall the hint of panic stirring. Then I turned a fraction, dislodging the pole from beneath my thigh; and at once my arm came free. Again I tried to sit up, pushing with my free arm now; to find that my head was locked. I reached up and over my shoulder – down, I suppose that should be –, and found that my rucksack was jammed beneath a sill of rock. I heaved, and partially freed it. Only for a torrent of water, previously dammed, to cascade over my face, stop my breath, and give free rein to panic. Had I lain there unheeding only moments longer the water would not only have washed away my guilt, but everything else besides: the bathwater, and the baby.

Blindly I reached for and released the chest buckle of my rucksack, then slid a shoulder from the strap. Only to have the pole jam it half way. But the extra freedom sufficed, for now I could move myself sideways far enough to pull the rucksack clear. I remember wondering that the evening had advanced so swiftly; then becoming aware, with renewed alarm, that I was still unable to sit up. To realise, a little belatedly for my self control, that my feet had finished somewhat upslope from my head. At which I swung my hips, and when, notwithstanding the poor light, I saw, rather than heard, my boots splashing into water, pushed onto my knees. I felt a twinge from the right knee, a small tug at my waist, and then a sudden parting, as I persisted, and righted myself. The rucksack fell snugly back into position, and at once the fullness in my throat decreased. Plainly I had been lying head down for so long that the blood had pooled to bursting point.

I remember, at that stage, supporting myself on outstretched arms and peering down to examine the rock I was kneeling against. It was a large, sharp-edged block of gritstone, and although washed by countless smoothing flows, still rough enough to rasp away flesh. I took off my trapper's hat, its fur fringe now soaking wet from my near-lethal immersion, and began to probe my skull. There was a definite sore area directly above the nape, but no swelling, no egg-shape. Nor did it seem as if the skin was broken, although that was more difficult to ascertain. But I could make out no blood on my fingers.

Turning to seat myself on the rock I searched a pocket for my paper tissues in their plastic bag and used the first few layers to dry inside my ears. Then I blew my nose, gingerly, and with care, but thoroughly enough to clear the nasal passages. After that, tilting my head, first to the right, then to the left, I held a dry tissue to each ear in turn. And was relieved to find, on peering into the paper, no sign of a discharge on either. And no blood. Or worse still, blood and clear fluid. I blew my nose again; and like any bogey-seeking schoolboy, peered even closer to see what I had got. To discover only the mucus I might have expected from a headcold. Evidently that too must have been gathering during my inverted siesta. And my eyes?

Carefully, only dully aware of my footfalls, feeling, rather than hearing my bootsoles strike against stones, I distanced myself a little from the rock I had come so close to denting, then focussed upon it. My head buzzed somewhat more than a little but the rock remained gratifying in the singular; I was not seeing double then. Only, on pushing back the cuff of my glove to peeringly consult my watch, I found the figures not that clear. Which left me to surmise that the thump my skull had taken had upset something in the visual field. And that did not augur well at all.

Having moved, however, I had at least found an explanation for the unduly-sudden waning of the light. It was not so much the lapse of time, for hardly fifteen minutes had passed since I had last checked, and that included the period when I had been lying comatose, lacking the will to move. It was mainly that I had been facing downwards, into the grough. Now, looking upwards, towards the sky, a pale afterglow of daylight was still discernible.

I considered the ache in my head. And notwithstanding that I could detect no bleeding, decided to play it safe, padding the bruised area with the rest of the tissues, then replacing my hat and tightly securing the chin strap, calling upon press studs never before used. In my rucksack I had more tissues. And some paracetamol. But loth to resort to medication I contented myself with palming up water and sluicing it into my face. On the other hand I was well aware of the dangers inherent in such a bang as I had suffered. In aviation the slightest head injury is reportable. Not that I had any intention of rushing to report this one. Not after so recently escaping from the clutches of the aviation-medicine establishment. Not if I could help it. Until two years back concealing information from the medics would have been an anathema to me. Now, already owing my career to doing just that, I had no intention of putting it into jeopardy again without far better cause.

I gathered myself, rather shakily, as I recall, and began to angle sideways up the grough. Only to lose all footing and slide down again at once, the rain having transformed the soot-like surface into grease. In the end I stumbled along the grough until a fall of boulders afforded easier footing, clambered up to the hag, then settled myself on the heather to take stock.

My right knee was what concerned me most. The ankle trapped by the peat had pulled free with nothing more than a twinge but the knee had obviously suffered a considerable wrench. At the moment it was merely sore but I had a mile or two to go still and I wondered how it would fare when put to the test. In my rucksack, apart from two more bags of tissues – for toilet emergencies; although heather, docks, and grasses had sufficed on many an occasion –, I had both a knee support and a wide crepe bandage, only it seemed too much trouble to unzip the top stowage to get at them. I did resolve, however, that should the knee begin to give me serious trouble I would press them into use. And if that failed to serve, I could splint the joint with a section from a hiking pole. As for my head, well, there was little more I could do about that. I pursed a lip at the rain-wreathed gloom. And again I consulted my watch. Only now I could no longer distinguish the figures, so, aiming to maximise what light remained, I stood up, bending my head closer to my wrist. To be assailed, on the instant, by an explosive roar within my ears. Then silence once again. As, unaccountably, I found myself face down upon the ground.

I lay there for some indeterminable space. My fall had been cushioned by the now-soaking heather, even so I do not think I actually passed out that time. Yet the unexpected collapse brought it home to me that I might be more shaken than I had realised. So I lay there, not exactly dazed, but not in any particular hurry to get to my feet. The tumble could have been due to general unsteadiness; in the nature of a faint. But I had to consider the likelihood of having suffered a concussion, or some complication even worse; though I took comfort from the lack of evidence of a discharge from the ear that might otherwise have hinted at some cerebral haemorrhage or other damage to the brain.

A simple concussion was much more likely, I reasoned, the boulder having rattled my grey matter in its bony box but done no further harm. Combat-survival first-aid told me that such a condition should not be too serious, not if I took things easy for a while. Only I had to move on. In which case this latest, quite unlooked-for fall would serve as a salutary reminder that, in my present state, in these weather conditions, and with full darkness almost upon me, it was more important than ever that I should watch exactly where I put my feet.

Fortunately, the task ahead of me was not too demanding. I must be within spitting distance of the edge path already. After which all I need do was try my best to avoid plunging over one of the crags, then locate the most convenient descent into Grindsbrook. It was later by far than I had planned to be starting down, nevertheless I still had ample time to get a train connection that night. Or failing that I could adopt my back-up plan and seek out accommodation in the Nag's Head, or the Ramblers'.

I remember deciding that it was hardly worth resorting to the compass, for that would mean getting the head torch out of my rucksack. Then too, my night vision had already accommodated to what light remained, while a bright torchbeam might make any visual damage even worse. And after all, as walking was a matter of taking one step at a time – rather like life itself –, it was enough that I could see the next few yards ahead of me. I pushed to my knees. The groughs promised the easiest way of progression. Without bothering to stand erect, therefore, I buttocked my way into the nearest of them, only this time taking the greatest care that I kept gravity well under control.

The lower joint of one of my poles, I discovered, was splayed out at such an angle that, initially, I doubted whether it would take my weight, and for just a moment I toyed with discarding it as a useless burden. Then, as from another dimension, Helen came to mind.

We had been watching a western. Or I had been watching; Helen had been steadily demolishing Super Sudoku puzzles, those with both letters and numbers. Our hero had upended his empty water bottle, then tossed it aside.

'So he's out of danger now.' I had awaited appreciation of my perspicacity.

Helen's head had come up, eyebrows raised, pencil momentarily stilled. Pausing, rather than waiting.

'Films always make them throw vital equipment away. For all he knows, there's miles more desert to cross. But even if he found water he'd have nothing to carry it away in. Basic survival stuff.'

'Darling, do shut up.'

I eased the kinked section into some semblance of straightness across my left thigh, jammed it up into the middle joint, then shortened the other pole to match. Standing, I satisfied myself that they were still plenty long enough. Then got under way.

I found the going surprisingly easy. For a good few yards the grough ran straight, and although it turned then, against the way I wanted to go, it soon turned back again, at least enough, I reckoned, to compensate and equal-out the error. In fact, my progress, for the most part shin deep in water, was more rapid than I might have hoped for, and as my boots splashed through pools and as I scaled mini-falls, sand-edged runs, and haphazardly-strewn, crazy-paved, gritstone steps, I recalled an initially-unseen party wreaking its high-decibel way up Grinds Brook. Full-throated shrieks and shrill shouts had seriously perturbed me, drowning out the very torrent's roar, until what

43

had come into view was not a catastrophe in progress but a safety-helmeted, stream-ascending gang of kids. The noise! But then, the fun!

Now, there was no such company; yet as I walked I was aware of a similar contentment, and although this was not a brightly sunlit afternoon, but a dusk-dogged, rain-lashed, mist-wreathed evening on a dreary upland moor, I did not feel in any way alone; and for all the drear surroundings, if any ghoul or ghost or hag or gremlin or goblin, unquiet spirit or soul unshriven had come my way they would not have been unwelcome; given that none of them sought to hinder my passage. For I had set up a rhythm steadier than any I had struck that day.

Nor did my physical state impair my progress, indeed I was no longer conscious of the ache inside my skull, while my right knee was the equal in strength to the other and even the damaged pole was behaving right manfully. On occasion I had to change from grough to grough and I remember scrambling hastily over the intervening hags as if only in the groughs could I keep up the pace I had settled to. And strangely, the pace I found I was setting myself was not merely faster than that I had set that afternoon but faster than any I had ever sought to walk at in the past. Besides, as always, in the groughs the air was warmer, and the rain less lancing. And I recalled with wonder my tiredness having reached the trig point, and the shock of that unnerving grouse. Since when I had tapped some inner source of energy, hitherto unknown; for now I had no need to rest, I was tireless, no marsh, morass, or hummock moor could wear me out, and the upland mere did not exist that, oppose me as it would, I could not conquer at a bound. And perhaps it was at that point that I fell again.

Chapter Nine

I know I remained conscious, for from the outset I had been aware of the chill on my cheek, pillowed on a mat of moss. And of the succeeding chill, prickling icily, as reality broke through the feyness I realised then had possessed me this last while. Then came the puzzling wonder that I should have fallen yet again. Until it registered that once more my unsteadiness had been presaged by a sudden burst of noise. Although what noise should have to do with anything mystified me equally. And though a notion stirred, it would not surface. Yet even then I recognised this latest amnesic retention as being in a different class to that tied up with colours. This fresh intangible, I knew – if I could only grasp it –, lay well within my own ken. Quite unlike the other. For what meaning could shepherds' markings have for me?

Wrists deep in the moss, its copious soaked-up moisture pouring into my gloves like so much dew, I pushed to my knees. Then, ignoring the tumult in my cranium, I unpopped my chinstraps and eased off my hat – again, not so much hearing the studs click apart as feeling them, I fancied, through my facial bones. The sodden hat clung tenaciously but I persisted until I could inspect, by what light lingered, the tissue-paper dressing it had kept in place. Any blood, I reasoned, would have shown up as a darkened patch, but all I could see was what appeared to be a pristine whiteness. My nose was running, and I sniffed. And sniffed again. Then, pinching each nostril in turn, I worked to clear the mucus, blowing only very gently, heedful of the thudding in my skull. After which, with knees awash, I plunged both hands into the moss, dashing my brimming palms, time and again, over both face and poll.

Realisation swept me then, that for some unaccountable time I had been walking, not to any purpose, not to any scheme, certainly not in any set direction, but as the whim had taken me. I pulled back my sleeve, but the protest from my skull overcame my need to check the lapse of time. And grateful as never before for the assistance afforded by the poles, I pushed to my feet, and straightened. That the knee would have stiffened by the next day to give me real gyp went without saying. But it would serve for now. I looked about me. The mist, already augmented by a decidedly fuller darkness, was all about me. Even had I had light enough I could not have seen a dozen yards.

But, I checked myself: a sure token that my mind was clearing! That last reflection belonged to the period of my feyness. For I had my head torch, of course. With the poles jabbed deeply home and my insteps now awash in water I steadied myself and swung my rucksack free. The zip of the lid, less used than most, proved momentarily perverse before delivering up the torch. Except that, probing with the finger of my glove, I found that both focussing-glass and bulb had taken the brunt of my headlong encounter with the rock. I gritted out a mild curse. But all was not lost! Unscrewing the remnants of the bulb I pivoted the main case to find the spare. And found instead the space it should have occupied. Then I cursed with feeling.

The throbbing in my head continued unabated, but this setback had yet further clarified my thought processes. My recent wanderings, I now realised, had not been directed by whim, so much as by the run of the groughs. Accordingly, I had no idea where I was now, not even whether I was closer to or further from the Edale edge than when I had started; nor had I any notion whether I had been heading towards Ashop Head, or the Downfall, or across towards Fair Brook and the Snake, or on towards Crookstone Knoll. And now the curtain of mist was there to mock my earlier regret that the visibility had been so fine. Once more I felt the stirrings of panic. Or better, call it alarm. But easy enough to stifle, the situation being one I had often conceptualised, not least in my one-time role as a combat-survival instructor. Indeed I had pontificated on the perils of Kinder to the lone walker earlier that very afternoon!

My gut feeling was that I was still closer to the Edale edge than to Fairbrook Clough. So I would revert to my original plan – made, after all, when there had been no pressure: the golden rule in all survival situations – and head for Grindsbrook, and Edale. Not that I would dignify being temporarily uncertain of my position – the air-navigators' euphemism for lost – as a survival situation. On the contrary, I had things well under control, and while I might not be able to make out the tiny figures on my digital watch I would certainly be able to interpret the compass. Only for the first time ever I regretted that the Silva model I had so parsimoniously invested in, while suitable for 'schools, scouts, beginners', did not run to a backlighting arrangement. I even remember grinning at my unashamed volte-face. And I remember even more clearly the grin fading as I pulled on the cord securing the compass to my belt. Only to discover at the end nothing but a sliver of plastic.

It had been that Lilliputian tug, back by the rock! Clearly the oversized hole I had drilled for security had weakened the base. And the irony of that was a stunner! For suddenly, without a compass; with visibility only a matter of yards; on a rainswept upland whose surface was to all intents and purposes level, so that few elevations offered an overall view even in daylight and good weather; with the blanketing cloud, so vainly wished for only hours before, blotting out even the few stars I might have recognised; my predicament had become decidedly unenviable. And as if to bring that home even more I became aware for the first time that hardly a scrap of my clothing was dry, and that a breeze which was not strong enough to disperse the clinging mists was more than sufficient to chill my core temperature. I shivered, my earlier ebullience and my cocksure conviction that I was familiar with and master of Kinder in all its moods vanished, 'gone with the wind' as surely as the poet Dowson's 'flung roses' and his Cynara's 'pale, lost lilies'.

Morosely, I kicked at a clump of moss. There was now a perceptible lump on the back of my head but still no bleeding. So after a moment's reflection I ripped away two large handfuls of the stuff, pressing and squeezing until I could wring them out no more. Then I replaced the tissues, moulded the sphagnum to my skull, and securing it with the hat, pulled down the earflaps against the breeze. Sphagnum moss had been good enough for the warriors of old. Now it would be good enough for a crass, overconfident, latter-day wimp like me.

I remember pausing to consider. Stupidity, or at the very best, misguided over-zealousness, had lost me my compass. But of course, the groughs would give me a clue to direction; away from the watershed their streams would flow towards one edge or another, and the closer to an edge they came the deeper the water would have carved the channel. It was only that as the night drew on I could see that I would get colder still and that the later the hour the less chance there was of finding accommodation once I did make it down to Edale.

Lifting a foot from the swamp it occurred to me that tree trunks harbour moss on their northern sides. And that would have been a handy directional aid six or seven thousand years ago before the sphagnum moss and those self-same ancient warriors between them had put paid to all the trees. Then again, one of Kinder's airmen-survivors had taken his initial fix on Edale from the glare of the briefly-exposed firebox of a passing steam train; except that, even given the visibility, today's diesel trains have no coal-fed furnaces.

Another scheme then. And this was a definite goer. Summoning every effort of will I forced myself to stop shivering, then, waiting until there was a lull in the breeze, strained my ears to pick up the faintest sound that might indicate a lorry, a motor bike, or even a train. But nothing disturbed the silence. I looked upwards. Air traffic into Manchester must have long since died away for I could not recall when I had last heard the whine of engines overhead. Yet even a high-flying aircraft pursuing its way along the Amber airways would have been enough. Only there was not a sound.

As I mulled this over I became aware that yet another irritant had begun hovering; this one on the very brink of consciousness. That it was something I would eventually have to confront, I was sure, only with hindsight I now believe that one of my defensive mechanisms was shielding me from facing it too soon. And so, even after getting under way again, I stopped from time to time, not so much to rest, although I was finding the going increasingly tiring, as to listen, always vainly, for the sound of traffic, air or ground, that would give me even a vague direction. And it was during the last such pause that this latest subliminal message finally bobbed to the surface. To drain the strength from my every sinew.

For minutes on end I had struggled with the most greasily precipitous grough yet, so that when I finally hauled myself over onto the hag and tipped onto my knees, I was panting heavily. I could see the exhalations issuing forth in clouds, feel the breath buffeting through my lips, feel my chest heaving, and the night air half-chilling, half-stinging my nostrils and the roof of my mouth; feel the blood pounding in my temples. I was aware of my shoulders, shuddering to the rack of a cough bidding fair to lift my cranium. I positively knew that I was puffing and blowing like a grampus; the noisiest grampus ever. And yet I could not hear a blessed thing!

I could see, but not hear, the rain gently soughing into heather; feel, but not hear, the ever-freshening breeze. I could absorb sensation through the soles of my boots, and through the bones of my face. Yet since that impact with the boulder, I realised now, my ears had picked up not a single sound.

I cannot, even thinking back, truly understand why this realisation that I had lost my hearing came as so telling a blow. Nor could I determine the levels at which my being responded to it, or why the response was so vigorous. But I was permitted scant time for reflection, for on the instant, the psyche hastened in to rationalise, and to attempt to reconcile.

'This loss of hearing,' it assured me, 'it can't more than temporary. So it can't affect your medical licence. And your eyesight is settling already. In fact, if it wasn't for the light you'd have no trouble reading the figures on your watch. You know your knee isn't seriously hurt, and neither your left leg nor your right arm have given any trouble at all. As for your mind, well, reasoning like this shows there's little enough wrong there. So what's a temporary loss of hearing going to cost you?'

And this last, at least, I could respond to. Reversing the query. What would temporary deafness gain me! To be shielded from the ubiquitous mobile-phone mouthings, from a whole youthful generation grown foul-mouthed, from public-transport chatterboxes. Not to have to mute-out TV advertisements … These would be positive blessings.

Perhaps, at this remove, it might seem obvious that I was not, in fact, functioning at quite the one hundred per cent the psyche would have had me believe. Then again my innate pragmatism had served me well after nightmare awakenings – another facet withheld from Helen. So, in this extremity, it had already persuaded me that the effects of the impact were indeed merely temporary, that even a brief rest, which I was presently denying myself, would cure them. Therefore, doubly protected against reality – faithful pragmatism having allied itself with seductive psyche, there was no logic in my morale deserting me.

Fear, without doubt, had breached yet more defences that – like those penetrated by Helen – I had hitherto believed sound. And others still, it seemed likely, that I had never known existed. But that my weakness might prove inherent was not the immediate problem. For the reality was that since my concussing fall I had gamely soldiered on, accepting every other tribulation and trivialising none; that up to this moment I had accepted the way my head was splitting; that the integrity of my eyesight had become suspect; that my knee was shooting painful darts with every strain I put upon it; that unaccountably, I kept falling. And always there had been the persistent nerve-draining dread that somewhere in the corrugated tissue of my brain, pressure might be building up, or fluid leaking out ...

All this I had assimilated lying back there by the boulder, and had mutely taken on board. Yet the confrontation with this deafness, posing nowhere near as serious a threat, coming as and when it did, weighed upon me like some final, resolution-sapping straw. The psyche had done its best. But it had been fighting rationality with trivia. And, deservedly, it had lost. All I could see, as I knelt there, was that for now, when it really counted, I was to all intents and purposes, stony deaf.

I do not believe, nevertheless, that at that stage, I ever considered giving up. Only, with the return of what I assured myself was rationality, I lost that ethereal lightness of spirit which had made my former progress so untroubled. Suddenly each foot became leaden, my right knee more voluble at every jolt, the moss compress of no more benefit than before. Gritstone boulders, such as I had just minutes earlier skipped over, became jaggedly insurmountable; and even the white-pebbled, sandy strands of groughs gave place to glutinous silt. Nor did another half-dozen falls help me husband what resolve I still retained, notwithstanding that each was directly attributable to the atrocious going underfoot. But then came a moment when, following yet another burst of near-excruciating sound, instantaneously curtailed, I found myself face-down again, my forehead grounding in the grough-side peat; and realisation broke upon me that things were far from good.

Not that resting there was unpleasant. I was out of the breeze. And I used the time to remind myself that in my rucksack was not only a dry fleece but a plastic survival bag – in essence nothing more than a glorified bin-liner, but orange, for easy identification. It was not much, but at least it was something I could crawl into until daylight gave me a chance of determining the shortest way to the succour I now admitted to needing. Only at that point, on top of the shivering, so deeply had the chill penetrated my dank clothing that I felt my teeth chatter. And suddenly, adrenaline-spurred, I sat up. No longer was the thought of reaching Edale merely attractive; it had become essential to my survival.

It was evident that, bin liner or not, being so cold and wet and woozy-headed, I was primed for exposure if benighted on the plateau. Even so it took me long minutes to get myself fully upright and on the go once more. It was chagrining enough to realise that I lacked that moral stamina on which I had always prided myself. Now, as I forced myself into motion, it was clear that I had also vastly over-rated my physical powers.

So what really kept me going, until I fell again, was not some welling source of will power, but sheer, unadulterated self-disgust. Primarily, of course, for having so overestimated my powers of both moral and physical endurance. But additionally for having so complacently underestimated the terrain, for venturing abroad with such a woeful stock of equipment, weather sense, and rusty know-how. It was a disgust to be reinforced, perhaps half an hour later, when I found myself struggling to my feet once more and realised that, having fallen on a patch of open peat, I was now facing I knew not which way, and with even less notion of which direction to take for Edale, or for any other edge.

That was not the last fall. But the next time that disorienting burst of sound overwhelmed my balance, I came to, not prone, but alean against the side of a grough, and although having suffered no further physical hurt, I was well aware that I had come dangerously close to my limit. Not that the sudden onset of this weakness surprised me overmuch, for I was well acquainted with the phenomenon by which shipwrecked mariners in lifeboats, airmen in dinghies, and the like, though physically uninjured, unaccountably give up, and passively drift into oblivion within a matter of hours.

I pushed myself upright, gritting my teeth, and grimly pressing on once more. Only to swim to wakefulness again, just a short while later – as I fancy now –, to find myself, face down this time, choking on a soupy, ice-cold mix of stagnant water, peat, and gritstone grounds. Awaking too, to discover that an immersed palm found no flow at all. Which told me that, for all my striving, I was further than ever from an edge, and back on the watershed. My lowered spirits sagged anew, nevertheless I lunged to my feet. But had the light been better, and had I looked, I might have seen the last of my morale slipping down into that peaty mire.

By now at least a part of me had begun to admit that the blow on the head had left my senses significantly more befuddled than I could, even yet, afford to own to. First-aid training had taught me that a simple concussion rarely has lasting effects. So I continued to attribute the longish-lasting symptoms I was suffering to being compelled to push on, rather than to take rest. At the same time I still took comfort from not having detected an aural discharge, placing a similar layman-like faith in the fact that I did not feel that I had cracked my skull.

Strangely, of the various effects that were distressing me, it was still the deafness that concerned me most. Would it really clear, I pondered, once I got down from the tops, and took some rest? Yet I could not discount the possibility of some damage to a nerve centre, as the result of cranial bleeding, for example. All I knew for certain was that I was rapidly falling apart; and mentally, rather more than physically. Except that minutes later, when I found myself facing the necessity of pushing to my feet once again, I knew that my physical strength too, had drained out through my boots.

I pushed up into a kneeling position. And there I stayed, a hopeless oppressiveness proof that I could go no further. I had simply run out of what the Finns call *sisu*; what boys' stories once called spunk, and thereby set us all giggling; what some might call bottle, or moral fibre; and what is probably best termed guts. No broken bone hindered my mobility and I had a reserve of energy food; more vitally, drinkable water abounded; only although my saliva was flowing freely there was not a gob's worth of defiance in me. And as I faced the realisation that I was indeed truly spent, the moss, gradually compressing beneath my weight, rose icily sodden around my knees. I looked up, registering dully that the rain, at least, was no longer falling. And it was then I saw the glow.

Chapter Ten

I cannot pretend that, at the sight of it, flickering indeterminately through the murk, my sinews instantly stiffened, that fresh courage immediately coursed my heart; or even that it furnished the arse-booting impulse my cravenness deserved; but suddenly I was on my feet again and pushing towards it, hardly daring to lower my eyes in case it disappeared. Had the notion registered that it was an ignis fatuus – a will-o'-the-wisp – perilously beckoning, I would have paid no heed. For so long now nothing in my surroundings had offered the least point of reference. Accordingly I had been blindly breasting through a woolly formlessness. Now, at last, there was something, insubstantial though it might be, to provide a focus. Polaris itself – 'I'm North, steer by me!' – could not have been more welcome. All I prayed was that it would not prove transitory, or move off before me as if it were, indeed, some impish marsh light. If only there was a moon! Then I could move quicker. But I knew, even as the thought formed, that the beacon before me was so frail that even the palest moonlight would have washed it from my sight.

What did come to mind, as I gritted my way onwards, was an RAF occasion when the moon, appearing not unlike this insubstantiality before me, had for moments on end, caused me almost preternatural concern. It too had started as a glow, then lifted, flamed scarlet, and paused, to crouch monstrously on the horizon, doubled in immensity by its reflection in the placid Mediterranean, losing all semblance to any natural body, but suggesting to a mind attuned to the politics of the day an atomic groundburst, blood red, menacing, and unearthly in the extreme. So that my co-pilot, returning from a periodical 'wings and engines' check, had stiffened, demanding shakily, 'What the bloody hell's that?'

I experienced no such bizarre feeling about my guiding star now, for unlooked for though its appearance had been, there was only momentary puzzlement. Earlier, dazed by my feet-aloft plummet onto that boulder, I had wandered off into feyness. Now, although my head still ached and my progress was ghostly by virtue of my inability to hear myself threshing through the mire, it was clear that this glow was anything but supernatural. It would be estate workers, rangers, shepherds – whatever! –, engaged in burning off heather, and obliged to stay until the burn was safe to leave; after far heavier rainfalls than today's the peat would still be tinder-dry a handspan down. Nevertheless I imagined how peeved the men must be that professional ethics committed them to staying so long on the tops; and more especially on a Saturday night. Not that I had regrets for them. My only concern being that they might call it a day and head homewards before I came up with them; they would hardly be overnighting up here on the tops.

Now truly infused with new-found vigour I found the going less strenuous than before, with relatively few, and then only minor, groughs. On the other hand, the ground was quite unutterably boggy, with rushes separating unexpectedly-extensive expanses of dark water. So broad, in fact, that I found myself doubting one of my long-held contentions and wondering whether Kinder really might contain some unfathomable Conan-Doyle-style bogs. This, however, merely allied itself with the rest of the night's experience to yet more fundamentally rock my convictions.

My pragmatism was untouched – that was unassailable – but my sense of self-possession had certainly been disturbed. So that a newly-adopted mantle of self-doubt made me cast wide circles around meres that I would earlier have splashed through with just a cursory probe of a trekking pole. Now, I trod warily. But never for more than the blink of an eyelid did I allow my attention to waver from the glow. It had become brighter as the thickness of mist shielding it from me diminished. And its colour had changed. Yellowish when first seen, it had then deepened towards amber; even reddening momentarily as a capricious air eddy stirred the curtaining vapours. And now, as I closed, so it gradually took on the spread of a wide-based conflagration. Yet, although I had the breeze in my face, I had not, so far, detected as much as a whiff of burning. So had the head-jolt disrupted my sense of smell too?

I paused, momentarily, and eyes levelled still, felt down to pull off a sprig of heather. In my samurai past I had often enough thanked my poor olfactory function when paratroops 'in a highly nervous state' – like Gilbert's policemen – were being upstanding for the drop. So with the headcold I had no hope. Nevertheless, 'An elusive little bouquet,' I quipped, although the words rang only dully in my head. And if it was not particularly amusing at least it represented my first essay into humour for some considerable time. So things were definitely looking up.

The glow, less diffused with every minute, had now become far more than just my lodestone. For although the night air remained chill it was as if its bite had been ameliorated by warmth and well-being. I began to peer ahead expectantly, hoping for some indication that I was in time. But apprehension grew too. Because although my progress, floundering through the marsh, seemed spirit-like to me, yet I had to be making more commotion than a dozen panicked sheep; only there was not a sign, so far, that anyone had taken note.

I splashed on, conscious that my boots were sending up wide sheets of spray, that gravel was rolling underneath my feet, stones tumbling and rushes swishing wetly. Only as a fringe of rocks took form to become an islet in the marsh and still no enquiring head appeared so the hope of succour that had soared so high within me, lost impetus, hung, then stooped, plummeting. It seemed I was too late, after all! That the men had judged it safe to leave. Possibly long since. Else anyone in the area would surely have craned towards my rogue-elephant approach.

I squeezed, knees sideways, between two boulders, clambered over several more, then splattered through another rushy mere, not yet ready to concede that I had missed the boat. And then, as I glimpsed their faces through a final fringe of rocks, I began to laugh. For although all were turned my way it was clear that neither alarm, nor undue curiosity, was a motivating force for anybody present.

I was in time, after all! Yet by the look of the fire it had been as close-run a thing as Waterloo. For although still burning with a fierce, almost metallic intensity close by, the greater part of its forty-foot length was no more than a mass of embers. Then too, the burn had been brought up by the largest mere yet, the scarlet and yellow flames, in reflection, suggesting that the water itself was on fire; just as an oily iridescence gave the illusion of great size and impossible depth. It was evident also, that the bordering rushes would be the burn's final fuel; unless the wind changed. And that it might do was clearly what had held the men so long. Bravo wind! I stepped up from the marsh onto a flat-topped rock and grinned down at them.

Chapter Eleven

Of the seven, six were in a loosely convivial group, sitting and leaning against rocks some twelve yards distant, while a loner had been seated beneath the one I had appropriated. Indeed, had he not risen to his feet and held out a restraining hand I might have put a boot on his shoulder.

'Sorry.' I felt my grin fade as I swallowed down something absurdly akin to a frog in the throat. 'Nearly trod on your 'ead.'

I caught the flash of his teeth, and saw his lips move, but that was all. Nor could I hear anything his companions called in greeting, some rising to their knees, others to their feet, to take in what, for all their former lack of interest, they must now view as, at the very least, an oddity. Yet surely, the thought occurred, there had to be at least one of them who had a superstitious streak. The one still lying back against his rock, for instance, now grinning. With relief? Not a hag or ghoul, then, not even a stampeding sheep – understandably not worth getting up to crane out at, but probably alarming enough, just the same –, merely a bedraggled and somewhat overwrought hiker only just managing to avoid clumsily booting one of their number. Suddenly embarrassed, I stepped to the ground, glad of the support afforded by a proffered hand, and began freeing myself of my encumbrances.

'Thanks!' I exhaled conversationally. Then realising that, unable to hear my own voice, I was probably bellowing, I endeavoured to lower the volume. 'Sorry! But can't hear a thing!' I tapped my ears, addressing myself to my aider and abetter. 'Only temporary, I'm sure. But I came a cropper back there. Banged my head.'

I unpopped the chin straps, and pulling off both hat and compress, turned the back of my skull to show him what I meant. The firelight, I was gratified to see, revealed no blood upon the compress. Gently feeling around, I found that although the bump had now swelled appreciably it was still far from the egg-sized dimensions of the comic books. I took my hand away, canting my head as his fingers probed in their turn, then looked up as he stood back; to catch his lips moving soundlessly once again. Realising that I was still having trouble hearing him, however, he raised a reassuring thumb.

I smiled with relief. 'No, I didn't think it was much. I suppose I should have sat down and rested rather than pushing on. But I wanted to get down before dark.'

He nodded understandingly, and turned to pass his report to the others; very likely I had couched my voice too low. One of them, a tall man, the only one still standing, raised an acknowledging hand and spoke a word or two to those about him. Whereupon the others turned their attention back from me to their own pursuits; to muttered conversation, it appeared, and staring at the flames; clearly they were as taciturn with strangers as most of their kind. For my part, now that I was in no pressing haste, I undid my rucksack, drew out my sit mat, and thankfully collapsed beside my neighbour.

'I couldn't be bothered to change before, but I've got a dry fleece in here.' I located it after a struggle, untwisted the white-wire tie, and slipped the garment from its protecting bag. 'What'd we do without plastic?' I was well aware that I was babbling, but found myself as powerless to control my tongue as to stem my shivering.

I shrugged out of my Gore-tex, then, chary of the lump on my skull, eased my soaking vest over my head. At this distance there was no appreciable heat from the fire, but moving closer would expose me to the breeze. Zipping the fleece to the chin, therefore, imparted a feeling of near-sybaritic luxury: a pussycat, so cosseted, would have purred!

I rattled on. 'Useless things, fleeces, aren't they, for doing anything strenuous in, but ideal when the work's over.'

He rubbed the material between finger and thumb, smiling as he called across to the others. Most turned their heads to grin, but the tall man, sitting alongside the rest now, merely nodded. Though appearing no older than the others he seemed somehow set apart.

'The boss?' I queried, in what I hoped was a low voice. And received both a raised thumb and an affirming smile.

Cautiously I shook my head, then eased a finger into each ear in turn, well aware of how easily eardrums can be perforated. Tentatively, I swallowed. But, as had been the case earlier that afternoon, there was no aural click; not so much as a relieving wheeze. As a second test I pinched my nose, and blew into it. Again, nothing. But that did not surprise me. When it comes to clearing the ears the world is split into the swallowers and the blowers, and ne'er the twain shall meet. My secret fear was that something more serious than my headcold was causing the deafness. Seeing my neighbour's quizzical expression, I told him, 'No – still solid.'

At least my headache was becoming less oppressive. Nevertheless, I took two paracetamols from the first-aid box, congratulating myself on the positive act. Before reaching the fire – my haven – such rucksack-delving had seemed altogether too much bother. Now I unscrewed my flask and poured a capful of blackcurrant, then, seeing my neighbour's interest, tendered it. He shook his head, reaching to examine the flask instead, peering into it, then running his finger over the deepest of the dents in the case. Very possibly picked up just this evening.

'Costly, but bloody sturdy, aren't they? Whereas those with glass innards break as soon as you look at them.'

Only I saw that he was talking with the others, holding the flask to the firelight, and had not heard me.

The hot drink, and the total cessation of stress, I suppose, set me on my feet again in no more than a matter of minutes. Just a short time before I had been appalled that such a minimal amount of privation could not only drain my morale but upset my mental equilibrium to the point where I had effectively given up. Now it was my resilience that surprised me. My headache was definitely ebbing, and my knee was no worse. Holding my wrist to the flames, I found that my vision, too, was sorting itself out. It was just that the digits were not that large. Very stylish and high tech. But pretty useless in these conditions. Grimacing, I mimed this to my companion who, grasping my sleeve, craned over the watch. Then, shaking his head, once more called across to the others.

Suddenly, without warning, that explosive roaring overwhelmed me once again, sending my senses reeling. Fortunately, sitting with my back against a boulder, there was no question of falling. More significantly, for just a moment, I heard a definite snatch of normal sound. It came from the other group where, I now saw, a more animated conversation had started up, one of them zooming his hand, palm down, through the air, and grinning widely. I caught nothing much. Just what registered as either, 'thing, Skip, whizzed,' or, 'thing, Shep, wizard.' That, together with the breeze keening through the rushes. Then the connection broke again, plunging me back into my world of silence.

It had been too fragmental, and too fleeting for me to grasp properly. But I had heard something! And that was enough to give the final lift to my spirits. 'Wizard', it might well have been. So was the whole world, then, talking about quiddage, and Harry Potter's broomsticks? Or swooping owls perhaps? For my part, I needed no magic. That burst of sound had sufficed. Now I was certain that there was no permanent injury; that given even more time and rest, my eyes would focus properly once again and my hearing return for good. As it was, the throbbings in both my knee and my head seemed to have lessened markedly, undoubtedly as the paracetamol kicked in. Above all there was comfort in the knowledge that if I needed physical assistance to get down to Edale there were willing hands in plenty to assist me.

That, however, was something I would go to all lengths to avoid. I had got myself into trouble up here, now the minimum disruption I caused to others, the better.

'I was going down into Edale,' I announced. Bucked up by the sounds I had just heard, I felt I could trust to my normal speaking voice once more. 'But I lost my compass, and I think the bang on the head disorientated me.'

To my delight, as I spoke the last few words, my left ear cleared, and I heard every syllable distinctly, if pitched oddly higher than I had intended. The ear went dull again at once, but now another connection made itself, this time in my memory bank. And the key was aviation-medicine. And now I had the explanation for my falling over.

As all flyers know, when there is a change in air pressure, any inequality across the ear drum is relieved by the excess air flowing away through an escape channel, the Eustachian tube. But the effect of a headcold is to thicken the mucous in the tube, hindering that relief. In extreme cases this can lead to the eardrum rupturing, although the air more normally very gradually leaks away. The inner ear, however, also contains the body's balancing mechanism, and should the release take the form of a surge of air, then the brain receives false signals. Which it impishly passes on.

'You're way off balance,' it says, straight-faced. And the subject falls over. Just as I had done.

My best guess as to how the condition had occurred in my case was that, as I had plunged head down onto the boulder, the resultant shock-surge had been trapped by headcold mucous. More certainly, in this instance the eventual inner-ear clearance had not occurred in one fell swoop but was releasing the air in fits and starts. And it evidently still had some way to go. But if the ears were reluctant to clear, the old cranium had been gratifyingly relieved of yet another of those plaguey subliminal irritants.

My admission that I had lost my compass seemed to have invoked another spirited discussion, and no little amusement. Without doubt, being in such intimate contact with the moors that were their workplace, the notion of having to depend on a compass really tickled them. Not that I minded. I was so grateful for their presence here that I would gladly have given any one of them my last Rolo. The discussion, after a few exchanges, was brought to a halt by Shep, or Skip – the gaffer, anyway. Lifting easily to his feet he nodded across the intervening space in our direction, addressed a few words to my neighbour, then waved away into the darkness, to my right. At once, divining what was intended, I glanced aside; to see that the other was already on his feet.

'You'll put me on the Edale path?' I asked.

Again, his lips moved, but he did not persist, shaking his head in a vigorous negative, instead. Then he pointed off over my left shoulder, in pretty much the direction I had come from. I inclined my own head, puzzled. 'Edale's that way? So I was going the wrong way?'

I sensed that one of the main group had called across to us, but beyond a slight frown my prospective mentor ignored the intended interruption, signing instead to my right, as the gaffer had.

'The Snake, then,' I said flatly. And tapped my forehead. 'I don't know my arse from my elbow.'

This too, seemed to meet with general approval; but it was a weird experience, to see lips moving and expressions changing, yet not to hear a thing. My designated guide, however, responded immediately, not only with a nod and a faint grin, but with a jerky, upraised thumb.

'OK, that's fine,' I told them, rocking my hand in an either-or gesture. 'Edale – the Snake, whichever. But the Snake'll do fine.' Yet how chagrining that my sense of direction had let me down so badly! But no time for self-recrimination. As in aviation, one erred, and moved on. Or rather –. I pursed my lips. That was how I might have expressed myself two years before. Now I would say one erred, and at one's peril failed to move on!

But even as a truism modified by hard experience, it was, at best, uncomfortable, and I swiftly put it aside. I was feeling full of beans. And once at the head of a clough I would not need light, compass, or forward visibility; just care. I would be an hour getting down, give or take. And there was bound to be a room at the Snake Inn; at worst, a corner to kip in. Rising with relative ease, I re-stowed my gear, put some fresh tissues beneath the moss-pad – good stuff, moss, no doubt, but potentially a bit mucky to put directly onto near-broken skin –, and having gingerly donned my wet shell, shucked on the rucksack. The fire seemed to be neither advancing nor dying out.

'You'll be staying a while longer then?' I called across to the gaffer, now alean against a boulder. He wore a white, roll-necked sweater, I saw, and had a moustache, thick and bristle-ended, where I might have looked for designer stubble. Nodding affably, he began to speak – precisely coincident with such a powerful wheeze from within my skull that I was convinced an ear was about to clear. But it was a false hope, and after a pause, seeing me shake my head, he contented himself with a smile, and a final wave, almost, the whimsy came to me, as if to a departing house guest. Two of the others had also lifted to their feet, and the other three, two kneeling, one still recumbent, waved in turn.

'Shep,' I mused, my mental picture of a shepherd having always been a man of age, white haired, and bearded. Another revision required! For of the six flame-ruddied visages turned my way all but the leader were clean shaven. All pleasant-looking, the firelight possibly revealing just a hint of tiredness behind their eyes; all young.

'Thanks for the beacon.' I indicated the fire. 'I hate to admit it, but I was way out.'

This admission too, seemed to catch the general fancy although some of the expressions, I fancied, seemed a little wry. And why not? I would be snug in the pub long before any of them! For good measure I indicated my assigned guide, 'I know I'm in good hands now, though.' An innocuous enough compliment, I would have thought, but not only did it dispel the wryness, it actually served to bring the house down. So much for taciturn! Ah, well! It was a great exit: always leave 'em laughing! I waved a pole in a second farewell and again every one of them responded, each in his fashion, some with waves, some with wide grins, the gaffer, this time, actually touching his temple in the semblance of a salute.

I had half-turned to follow my guide when a stocky bantam of a lad who had been kneeling by the recumbent member of the group shot to his feet to grin hugely as he called something across to my companion. Just as the sound curtain gave another twitch.

'Take care, Jack, red on ...'

I heard nothing else, but aware that my guide had tensed, I turned, to surprise a sudden ruddiness of his cheek that owed nothing to the fireglow. I guessed at once that the sally had been barbed, also that it had gone home; but the recipient – Jack, evidently – merely shot a glance at me, then led off into the darkness. Minutes later, docilely trailing in his footsteps, I took the opportunity to turn and look back. But the mist had closed in behind us and already there was no sign of the fortuitous – the serendipitous, perhaps? – will-o'-the-wisp glow that had served me so incredibly well.

To find myself trailing to someone else's lead imparted a strange sense of being protected: *shades of being snug in a pram, would you say, Helen, with rain pattering on the hood?* During that so-unsettling training flight it had not been rain, but doubts, pattering down. Yet suddenly I found myself possessed by the strongest presentiment that future flights would hold no such doubts.

The assurance welled up, ready formed, from my subconscious. It fell far short of furnishing the relief from guilt I craved, but offered, at least, a pragmatic way forward. The lesser element of my doubts, I could now see, had been little more than a lassitude of spirit as I had relaxed from the intensely emotional 'Will they, won't they, clear me medically' turmoil of the last two years. This, it was evident, would disappear with the signing of my licence. Far more problematical was fighting the guilt feelings surrounding my return to carrying dependent, trusting, passengers and crew once again; that was a battle I would have to win on every flight. To succeed would require me to mentally compartmentalise my operation. And only time would tell if I could bring that sort of moral strength to bear.

But as a walker too, it was out of character to find myself trotting at another's heels; the recent debacle notwithstanding. Just the same, had I been able to hear Jack's replies I would have used the time to bombard him with questions; after all, it was not often one found oneself a tame moorland denizen! They were clearly not Peak Park Rangers, but as general estate-workers did they double as shepherds? Or was it the other way around, were they primarily shepherds? As it was, although I did ask a question or two, and although my hearing did relent on occasion, it was never more than a momentary remission, and I eventually gave up. The question I was simply bursting to ask could wait until we reached the path.

Gradually, as we passed further from the fire, so my eyes accommodated once again to the night. Until abruptly the heather and bilberry underfoot gave way to sand, and a matter of yards later to a score of rutted footprints. These swiftly braided into a main pathway which initially crossed our direction of travel then vanished into a shadowy declivity. I took another step or two, then looked up. To find my companion lagging. Pointing downwards, he inclined his head questioningly. I nodded, grinning. For the first time in who knows how many hours the big 'I'm-so-at-home-on-Kinder' actually knew where he was! 'Fair Brook – Fairbrook Clough,' I mouthed.

He grinned back at me: I could see the contours of his face change. A very slow grin. Then he nodded, and gave me a valedictory thumbs-up.

'Thanks,' I said. 'I'll be fine from here.'

The parting of the ways. But I was afraid that, being in the mould of taciturn men, of John Wayne and that ilk, he might simply slouch away. And there was something I was desperate to establish. Only at that moment he reached out as if to shake hands. Readily, I pushed out my own. To find that he was not offering so much as proffering. And I recognised the plastic-wire tie. He twisted the ends together, eyed the result, and unfastened it again. Then, wordlessly, but with a nod of appreciation, placed it in my hand, and turned away.

Though intrigued, I had something much more urgent on my mind.

'It's Jack, isn't it?' He paused obligingly enough, inclining his head in acknowledgement. 'Maybe I can leave your crowd some drinks at the Snake? You saved my bacon, after all.' He smiled then, and with a certain wistfulness, I fancied, but shook his head, and once more went to turn away. But I had to get to the bottom of that obviously provocatively-shouted exchange back at the heather-burn.

'Jack, that chap back there –' I began. Only, as I lifted my chin interrogatively, so the roaring once more filled my ears. My world was tilting, but I was determined not to fall this time, grasping at his shoulder for support. And so we stood, with him acting as my prop, for perhaps thirty seconds, until my equilibrium had come back to kilter.

What very slightly piqued me, as we waited, was to discover that, in contrast to my extremely expensive Gore-tex, his leather biker's top – both its bulkiness and its sheepskin lining reminiscent of the old Irving flying jackets – showed no trace of dampness. Natural animal oils, *dix points*; man-made technology, zilch! Tentatively, I stepped back. To find that my world stayed level. Although any hope that this latest turn might have totally cleared my hearing was dashed on the instant. For Fair Brook, just feet below, was foaming with white water, but still I could not hear a thing. I pitched my voice to overbear the clamour that must have been booming all about us, and tried again.

'Jack, that chap back there – he yelled out something, just as we left.'

The other's arm, still outstretched in case I needed further aid, dropped. We were much of a height, and standing in such close proximity I could not miss the sudden uneasiness in his expression. I craned yet closer, to catch any movement of his lips.

'It was something about "red".'

He shifted, his discomfort clear now. But I persisted, grasping at his arm again. 'I fancied it was "red on" something.' But then bit my lip. What a pointless initiative! Being effectively deaf, I had to force 'yes' or 'no' responses; a nod, or a headshake, something I could see. 'Was it,' I blurted, '"red on – blue"?'

As if stricken, he pulled his arm free and stepped back. His expression was unfathomable, but I felt certain that had he replied it would have been reproachfully. As it was, set-shouldered, and rigid with hurt, he simply turned, and strode off into the darkness, passing from my crestfallen gaze like some spectre returning to the night.

For a moment I thought of attempting to catch up with him, to explain about the worm that had for so long been niggling at my mind. But I was not yet up to a sudden sprint. Nevertheless I waited for a minute or two, peering through the mist in the hope that he would turn back and give me a chance to explain. Not that I thought he would. That sally back there had cut him. He must surely have felt that I, too, was using him as a butt. Only there was nothing I could do about it now. In the end, I hunched my rucksack higher, and set myself to the descent. I felt like a dog who has not just bitten, but bitten off, the hand outstretched to feed him. And even then, I had resolved nothing. The word I had supplied might not have been 'blue.' Indeed it was highly unlikely that it had been. And even if it had been, then it would still have signified absolutely nothing to me.

Chapter Twelve

Like many cloughs on Kinder, Fairbrook falls away from the edge in a close-to-vertical tumble of boulders. Such rock ladders look daunting both from below and above, but they never present a problem even to the most pathbound of walkers, offering, as they do, an infinite variety of routes through them. My normal method of undertaking steep descents is to employ my fully-extended poles as banisters, setting them well below and gradually letting them bear my weight as I gently re-plant my fairy feet. In this instance, the darkness precluded that, and instead, it had become a question of descending backwards, poles dangling on their straps, securing at least one hand hold, then lowering a foot until I found a firm, if unseen, surface in the murky depths below. It had not been a hard descent, even then, but care had demanded that it be a slow one.

Because of the earlier rain it had also been, of course, a wet one, for in this early stage the line I chose was the actual bed of the infant Fair Brook. What had taken this stream-bed-descent out of the ordinary had been that the torrent, boiling past me in pale rushes, had done so as soundlessly as so much cotton wool. Some distance down I had smacked a sizeable stone against a rock, but although I had felt the impact, as I had felt the heave of my breathing, and the mouthing of my occasional curses as a stone turned underfoot or a pole point slipped, not a sound had come through.

I had been sniffing frequently by then, resorting to gentle, fingered-nostril clearing when I had a hand free but avoiding any hefty snorts which could initiate the go-stop pressure release; I could do very nicely, thank you, without an equilibrium upset while I was transferring my balance from one chisel-edged rock to another.

My headache, for its part, had faded by then to the mildest of throbbings, while my knee had been holding out well. It was, I had reflected, as if the glow of that so-serendipitous fire was about me still – I had now acceded unashamedly to Horace Walpole's word, coined in the eighteenth century and become suddenly cult in the twenty-first – for during the whole descent I had never lost this feeling of being cosseted, of walking in someone else's footprints.

I had anticipated that the going would be easier below the rock ladder; but I had not allowed for the darkness. There had, indeed, been long stretches where the path had been relatively unencumbered by obstacles, and although the cloud blanket had been so thick as to preclude the faintest glimmer of a star, some faint luminescence had been evident. But this had only created a false impression, masking how little light there actually was. For whereas I had been clambering down, with sloth-like caution, from boulder to boulder, my tendency on these easier parts had been to quicken my pace, cast aside care, and blithely stride the half-seen, half-sensed delineation between pale, boot-trodden way and dark heather. Blithely, that is, until the first time an underfoot rock sent me tumbling.

In truth, most such upsets had been stumbles rather than tumbles, but they had invariably occurred when I had unwarily swung back into a rhythm rather than taking it one tested step at a time. Slow, I had eventually conceded, though frustratingly time consuming, was sure. And once I had re-learnt that lesson I had made, if not quicker, then certainly less painful progress.

Just the same, it had been a boot snubbing a rock that had brought me the first intimation of change. I had realised that I had not just felt the impact but had actually heard the thud of leather; and this without any unsettling of my gyros! I had tried a repeat performance at once, kicking at the rock time and again. But that had not been the way it was to work.

Where Fair Brook is swelled by the becks issuing from Upper Seal and then Middle Seal Clough, there is one of Derbyshire's most picturesque waterfalls. On this descent the darkness had hidden it from me, but although not conscious of hearing anything I had suddenly become aware that it was nearby! From then on my recovery had become an exciting progression, a delectation to be savoured like a good port, a joyous return to normality in which each fresh, burp-like pulse of sound, like every studied pace, had served to shorten the distance to go, to soften the path underfoot.

As I had passed Nether Seal Clough I had discovered that I was able to hear a whistle when I pursed my lips and blew. Not a particularly clear or tuneful note, but then the ability to whistle is a lifelong non-accomplishment, and one much regretted throughout schooldays.

Then, just before negotiating the forded junction with the path from Gate Side Clough, passing once more onto grass, and glad of its whiteness to show me where the track deviated from the brook, I had clapped my hands, and had not only heard the smack of palm on palm but, a heartbeat later, the scrabbling as a startled sheep went crashing upwards through the bracken. And having reached the River Ashop footbridge I had dallied by the gorge for minutes on end, greedily drinking in the roaring of the waters as they girded themselves to boisterously welcome Fair Brook, deserted by me but joining the main flow just a few more yards downstream.

The slope up to the Snake Inn from the bridge is not particularly hard going, but it is invariably cluttered; or at least, it is following the way I choose to take. This is a diagonal climb through the fringe of the Snake Plantations, directly towards the Inn. And although it is invariably boggy and trackless, with interlacing snares of rotting pine and thorn-laced bramble, the alternative is the regular footpath which makes a shorter uphill transit but then marches for some distance with the A57; the trunk road being the venue, by both day and night, for boy racers of all ages to pilot juggernauts through the tortuous twists of the Snake Pass.

On the other hand I had once found peril enough in the off-path route, having come across a distressed ram firmly horn-snagged in the ruins of a stock fence. Had I not chanced to happen along its hours would have been numbered. Arguably, just as mine might have been back on Kinder, had it not been for the estate lads! But like them I had played the Good Samaritan-cum-shepherd, and crouching low, had laboured to set it loose. To receive, as sole reward, an eye-blacking backward head-butt as it had frantically scrambled free. A reward, I reflected wryly, not unlike the ingratitude poor young Jack had received tonight.

Nor had the wood been inclined to permit me free passage this time either, and neither the rumble of a passing lorry on the road above nor the fading clamour of the river below had drowned the strident, 'Bastard! *Bastard* thing!' I had tendered as barbed wire had ripped across my shin. My hearing, at least, I had been able to reassure myself, was well and truly back.

Feeling down with bared fingers it had been clear that the gash was bleeding freely; but there had been little to gain by trying to staunch the flow then and there. Instead, I had doggedly pressed on, past bodily prised-out tree roots that had reared before me like dark starbursts, until eventually I had picked up the glare of sodium lights playing on the Inn's end wall.

Pushing my way laboriously up the steep, grass-hummocked and rubbish-strewn embankment immediately below the road, hitherto-unsuspected tensions had dropped from me as I saw lights in all the windows. First the succouring heather-burners, and now our kindly host awaited; it had indeed been my lucky, lucky night!

What had struck me, as I had negotiated a wire fence to access the road, had been the fresh face the old place had assumed since I had last visited eight years or so before. It had even changed its name, I fancied. What I recalled as the plain Snake Inn had now become The Snake Pass Inn, as evidenced by Tolkienesque mural of vines and hops; although the landowning Cavendish family's rearing snake still found its place. Then, directly beneath the art work, the bright globe of a replica oil lamp had beamed its welcome through a window; all the weary traveller might have looked for on passing 'across the ford and up the steep path' towards Elrond Halfelven's Last Homely House, shining as the Snake Inn does 'in the midst of beautiful woods and' if not exactly 'just in the shade of tall mountains' then certainly in the shadow of some high and misty hills.

I had paused at that point, smiling somewhat, reflecting that if I could get thoughts as picturesque as that down on paper, Helen for all her first, and the doctorate that had followed, might soon be quoting me rather than Shakespeare. Or, for that matter, the Wilde chap she had recently slipped in just to confuse the issue and do me down.

The no-drink-and-drive culture had meant that there had been few vehicles in the car park. Not the first blow to trade suffered by the now-venerable Inn. For only a short while after metamorphosing from Lady Clough House to serve the last of the great road-improvement enterprises of the early nineteenth century, the Glossop to Sheffield Turnpike, it had lost much of its business to the even newer Manchester to Sheffield railway to the north, only recovering, and but partially at that, with the influx of moorland visitors seeking grouse to slaughter, and that new vogue, Gothic scenery.

My historical reverie had been brought up short as I had found myself confronting a Land Rover of the RAF's mountain rescue service. An encounter which had instantly flooded me with ambivalent feelings, the overriding one of which had been mortification at having so nearly become yet another rescue-service statistic. Just the same, my first admitted-to sensation had been relief at discovering that the legend stood out in clear definition, even when shielding off each eye in turn; although I had reserved judgement on that head until I could re-run the test on smaller letters.

My main concern had been to deal with my conscience. For as a declaration-of-intent the big outdoor man had told Helen only that he might go to the Kinder area. Which probably ruled out Lathkill, and possibly Dovedale, but little enough else. For misadventure, read sheer overweening arrogance! But the most sobering of considerations had been that, prior to finally alerting the authorities, Helen, always more attuned to my overburdened state of mind than I was myself, would have been left to suffer hours of unrelieved concern.

To my shame, however, as I had turned towards the porch an incorrigible egotism had displaced all altruistic contrition, reminding me that mountain rescue teams often had a doctor on their strengths. If that was the case here, I had realised, he might look at my shin. After all, that barbed wire might have been rusty, or infected with who knew what. And with the age's new infections, blood has become such funny stuff. After which, purely in passing, of course, I might bring to his attention the bump on my skull ...

I had spent a minute or two by the porch steps where I had re-hitched my pants, added mud to more mud by rubbing my boots against my trouser legs, stowed both cap and the moss-and-tissue padding, and smoothed back my hair. I had once calculated the cost of my walking ensemble at only a little less than a thousand pounds. Yet as a fashion plate I fail dismally. Not least because where others pass over peat bogs with mud-caked boots I acquire mud-caked thighs. The old hostelry had grown accustomed to itinerants of all sorts over the ages but anyone so closely resembling Schultz's Pigpen had far better take precautions.

One other thing I had done. I had retrieved my Ministry-approved reading glasses from my Gore-tex shell, wiped them to some semblance of cleanliness, then bent and perused the examples of acceptable plastics displayed by the door, grunting with satisfaction when I found I could read even the tiniest character. My composure had suffered a severe jolt, however, when I had glanced to the right, to find a decidedly tacky plastic thermometer; overlooked, surely in the refurbishment! An instrument that registered positive temperatures above the datum line, negative below. Positive in red. Negative in blue. Red on blue! I had shaken my head; finding this just a little too much. Then I had pulled myself together, and opened the porch door. I had just experienced an adventure. And like all adventures it was already proving infinitely more agreeable now than it was over than when it was under way.

Chapter Thirteen

I had entered into a warm, weatherproof sanctum, redolent of sawn pine and wax floor polish, in which the night chill had no place; although the Arctic conditions that can obtain on the Snake Pass were graphically shown by some photos in the lobby. Milk and honey had come to mind – albeit in the form of Draught Guinness and scampi with chips –, the overall feeling having been one of coming home.

And this despite remembering that on my last sojourn I had entered into a wrangle with the landlord because my room had no serviceable lock, and suffered my first ever excruciating après-coup leg-cramp whose recurrent spasms had seen me writhing on the bedroom floor for a good half hour, despite having luxuriated beforehand in a hot bath. Much renovation work had been done since, however, and having remarked upon this it had come as no surprise to discover that, in the interim, the enterprise had passed into new hands.

My bedroom had been smartness itself and I had avoided banging my head on the lower of the two beams running the length of the sloping roof; moreover the door had been lockable, and I had been given a key! Downstairs again, I had also had to turnabout my memory of a spit-and-sawdust public bar. It might well have been the same bar counter, its dark wood reflecting what it could see of a blazing fire, but gone was the former starkness, instead, the whole room, with its pictures, ornaments, and trimmings, had radiated cheer.

In past years there had been a molten component from some Kinder air-crash on a shelf. No longer. But I had taken advantage of the barman's occupation with a repeat order to re-check my close vision against the various fonts of the 'Consumption by persons under 18' notice. I had walked a few steps back, and equally-closely examined the bare-fist bruiser posing to one side.

And finally convinced that my eyes had recovered, I had considered the sepia prints of early Snake Pass motorists who, by the look of them, were as hair- and care-raising as their modern counterparts.

'Sir?'

I had looked around, smiling. A good start! Sir, not Mate.

'Ah! Thanks. Draught Guinness, please. A handled glass?'

The dimpled body snug in my palm – why, habitually ignoring the handle, do I bother asking for a tankard? –, I had gazed around me. There had been three men just about to leave. I had judged them to be weekend-working businessmen who, by the evidence of their thoroughly-scoured plates, had just enjoyed meals. There had been two more men in a corner, chattily idle as they had settled to their newly-replenished drinks, and a married couple; or at least, married, going by the studied silence between them.

Then there had been an older chap, a grey-bearded, ruddy-cheeked Derbyshire hillman, I put him down as, who, by the gnarled look of him, might never have ventured beyond Buxton. Just the same, as things were these days he would undoubtedly prove to have business interests world wide, to regularly visit equally far-flung offspring, and presently be unwinding having just jetted back from his Spanish villa. Or not. However, my attention had already switched itself to the noisy group thronging the end of the bar, effectively blotting out both the fire and access to the dining room. The story one of them had been telling would have served as introduction, had that been necessary.

'Looking down at the pilot's body, one of the team says, "You know, it's ironic, but it's this guy's twenty-first today." And so they all linked hands and danced around the wreckage singing, "Twenty-one today, twenty-one today" …'

It had gone down well. As it always had done. Probably true enough too, though arguably apocryphal. And the characteristic black humour also, had been as deceptive as ever. For it had been clear that none them were hard cases. Or not as such. Physically, they had tended towards the stringy rather than the muscular. Possibly only their haircuts had set them apart from any other group of their age, short hair – though not skull-scraped – being as sure an identifying feature of the Serviceman as ever it had been seven years back, when I had put aside blue-grey tunic for a dark-navy jacket.

It had become evident that they had just completed an exercise on Bleaklow and had called in for a meal on their way to another, to be held next day on the Howden Moors. And there had indeed been a doctor. Or so I had deduced, from his ready response when addressed by the others as 'Doc'.

On shucking off my rucksack upstairs I had taken a cursory look at the cut on my shin, and having ascertained that it was about six inches long, and that it had clotted, had deliberately left it as it was. At this point I had carried out a further, surreptitious check, to find that when I eased my sock away from the clot the blood started welling once again. Quite apart from the dried, red-brown runnels, my shin had been far from clean, and as there had really been no saying what might have been on the barbed wire, it had been case of the sooner I had it looked at now the better. Notwithstanding which I had bided my time until 'Doc' had declared that he was off to 'pump out the bilges' and pushed free of the group. I had waited for a decent interval, then, not without a certain amount of trepidation, had followed suit.

'Doc' had just been rubbing his hands under the hot-air dryer when I had pushed through the inner door. 'Sorry, sir, for doing this –.' Aiming to strike a balance between a facile approach and an unabashed apology I had pulled up my ripped trouser leg and displayed the gore-soiled limb. 'But as you've not keeled over with 'orror you probably are a doc, Doc.'

It had smacked of asking a solicitor for free advice at a party, but I had been in luck, for he had smiled.

'What was it? A bramble?'

'Barbed wire,' I had told him. 'I wondered if the wire might be rusty. It was too dark to see.'

Giving his hands a final brisk rub, he had nodded at a radiator, 'Bung your heel up there, sir.'

Gratefully, sir had done so. No trouble for Darcey Bussell. Uncomfortably high for sir.

Moments later, 'Hang on here,' the doctor had directed. 'I've got my stuff outside.'

I had gone through the motions of demurring, but he had walked briskly off, returning a minute or so later carrying a rucksack that had showed signs of much use, also a round-topped stool. 'Squat on this.'

After some practised ministration he had decided that no stitches were called for, but had stuck three flesh grips across the cut before applying a bandage. 'It's clean enough now,' he had said, rising from his knee and walking to the basin, clearly preparatory to returning to the bar. I had thanked him, as I too had stood up. 'There was something else, Doctor. I hope you don't mind ...'

I had been relieved when, instead of looking pointedly at his watch, he had simply waited, quietly courteous. And so I had launched into my tale, the bang on the head, the subsequent unsteady spells; the blurred vision and the loss of hearing, the brief rest, and the eventual recovery of both faculties. He had heard me out without interruption, and then, moving the stool directly under the strip lighting, had beckoned me onto it again. For the next space of time I had simply done what I was told. Largely it had been a matter of him probing – not that gently, either – at my sore skull; using some torch-like device to peer into my eyes – he had spent a long time over that –; and another, I fancy, to examine my ears. Throughout the inspection he had kept up a series of questions, not all of them medical. I had tacitly admitted to 'working in the city'.

'Weekend break from the rat race, eh!'

He had laughed at the notion of my trig-to-trig exercise; without doubt his time in the hills was far more productively spent.

'How long would you estimate you were unconscious for?'

Three minutes, I knew, was held to be a critical period. It was something else I had taken comfort from on the moor.

'My best guess, Doctor, is not more than a minute or two. I believe that, for most of the time, before I got to my feet, I was more in a daze. And after the first time, I don't think I actually passed out at all. I feel that, had I rested …'

There had already been a couple of interruptions during our impromptu clinic. The first to enter, edge past, and two minutes or so later to leave in the same way must have been a stranger, I imagine, for in true English fashion nothing had been said. The second, however, entering when I was intently eyeballing the light, had clearly been one of the team.

'Typical! Bloody officers all the same. Your round, and you skive off in here doing your Flo Nightingale act.'

'Piss, Mickey,' the doctor had returned equably, 'then piss off.'

There had followed a minute or so of whistling, the drag of a zip, and again the sense of someone edging past before the door had closed on a laugh.

A short time after that I had become aware that the door had opened once more, but by then the doctor had had me directing my gaze ceilingwards again.

'Good thought, that moss! Though to get any supposed antiseptic or drawing benefit I suspect the ancients would've applied it directly to the affected area. Who knows! But I agree, losing your compass like that wasn't the best of tricks.'

'What really shook me, Doctor …'

And I had told him of my chagrin at the way the heart had gone out of me. In truth, I had welcomed the chance to even partially unburden myself on that score, for the knowledge that I had so little mental grit, I had known, would take me a long time to come to terms with. More especially as I would be unable to confide in Helen.

'I just couldn't believe how quickly I came to the end of my tether, Doc. Honestly, I really believe that if it hadn't been for a heather burn …'

I had gone on to tell him how the mere sight of the fire had lifted my spirits. And of the benevolence that seemed to have surrounded me from then on.

'Or at least,' I had striven for a manfully-wry finish, 'until I wrapped myself about with that bloody barbed wire.'

He had laughed. Then tapped me on the shoulder. 'Right,' he had said, beginning to re-pack his rucksack, 'you'll do.'

I had straightened up. And had realised that the other occupant of the room, now just giving a perfunctory shake at the nearest of the two urinals, was the old country lad from the far end of the bar. Momentarily catching his eye, I had nodded acknowledgement, turning aside again as the doctor had commented, 'They were burning off heather towards Black Hill, too, despite the rain. And they say it'll be even wetter tomorrow. Anyway –,' he had shoved out his lower lip, 'a good night's rest should sort you out. But it wouldn't be a bad thing to get yourself checked out when you get home. Give 'em the whole story.'

'I'll do that, first thing,' I had promised, temporising even as I had done so that a partial mental reservation was neither graceless nor dishonourable. I had held open the door for him, 'And thanks a bunch, Doctor. I'll take the stool back.'

He had given a half salute, nodded familiarly to the old man, and left. For my part I had lifted the stool to the side of the room, out of the way, and moved towards the cubicle, nodding in my turn as the old man had passed. And a little later there had come the sound of hearty farewells, cut off abruptly as the porch door closed. Ensconced in the cubicle I had sighed. It had been, quite literally, a day of ups and downs. But meeting the estate chaps back up on the tops, and the doctor down there in the pub, had meant that the ups were most definitely ahead of the downs; and by a very long way at that.

Chapter Fourteen

In the course of ordering my meal I had quizzed the barman about the piece of aircraft wreckage formerly on display and had learnt that the new owner, considering it gruesome, had passed it on to some air-crash enthusiasts. But aviation had still retained a presence, for from my table I had been able to see two small representations of Lancasters engaged on the Moehne Dam operation, while a picture of an American Superfortress brought to mind the near-obscene amount of debris that had lingered on Bleaklow's Higher Shelf Stones, certainly until just over two years back. What I had viewed with unreserved appreciation, on the other hand, was the sly humour and the gratifyingly-sound scanning of the 'The Pennine Poser' verse hanging nearby, being complacently assured that no one would take me for a poser. Or not if they caught sight of my peat-mired, and even bloodstained, pants.

With my meal finished, and before deciding whether or not to order a second pint, I had checked my watch. By now, I had decided, Helen would have been back at home, leaving her early-evening clients to wrestle with their newly-unlocked traumas. High time to make that call!

I had used the red, steam-technology public phone box outside the building. For some time now I had been mulling over just how much to tell Helen. Not everything, that was for certain, for to do so would be to set her worrying every time I ventured out of doors. However, telling her of my resolve to cast aside my apprehensions where we were concerned could wait no longer.

She had evidently been expecting the call, but I had quickly established that I had caused no concern by not having got in touch earlier. Yes, it had been an enjoyable walk. And profitable. To a certain extent, at least. No, I'd found myself running late, and as she was tied up tomorrow, I'd decided to overnight.

I had taken advantage of these preliminaries to get my brain in gear, so that by the time we had approached the nitty-gritty I had pretty well decided what to broach, what to leave unmentioned. But, in part, Helen had pre-empted me, and in doing so had shifted my focus from the evening's drama. And just as well, for otherwise I might have told her more than discretion dictated. Before leaving home I had asked her to drop in and check my answerphone, just in case I decided to overnight. A precaution that had paid off.

'Crewing left a message. Your next refresher flight's at eleven on Tuesday morning.'

I had digested that. And had actually found it good! It also gave my headcold time to clear. I had been aware that Helen was giving me a moment for reflection.

'How do you feel about that?'

'You know, as strange as it sounds after my whining yesterday, I feel fine. But Helen, about giving up the flat, I've decided –'

'Tell me about the flying first, Mark ... You feel good now, you say?'

'I really do. I'm not quite sure what to put it down to, but I suspect the fresh air and all has cleared the cobwebs. I can only liken yesterday to a kid spending weeks looking forward to a party, then having a tantrum about going. That sort of thing. And, well, not forgetting all the other real stuff, of course.'

'Uh-huh.' Helen's interjection had hung there for a very long time.

'Yes, I'm convinced that's all it was. Now I feel absolutely fine about getting airborne again. I can't wait, believe me. But anyway, about the flat ...'

'Look –' Having caused me to break off there had been a long pause. It had been clear that she had fallen into one of her studies. 'So you actually managed to think it through then, as you were walking? The flying, that is. Is that how it happened?'

I had relaxed. Although until that moment I had not realised just how tensed up I had been. But despite Helen's evident suspicions there had been no sign of dangerous ground in the offing. For although she had been delving, that was what she always did. Besides, it had been surface stuff. And I had never had problems at that level.

'No, as I suspected, I'm a complete berk at thinking things through – pardon my language. But I suppose scrambling about today gave me some sense of proportion. Osmosis! That's the process. I didn't really get started on thinking. But I suddenly realised, selfish or not, I just can't let that woman go. And then, or just a little later, it was as if the flying too had clicked into place.'

'As if something had released you, would you say?'

My alarm klaxon had suddenly gone off into overdrive, my very own built-in cockpit voice-alert. 'Pull-up! Pull-up! Terrain! Terrain!' Clearly I had relaxed just that shade too much. But then Helen did that. She snuck in. And this was dangerous ground indeed! High terrain, and cloud covered at that!

At a guess I might suppose that it had taken my near-escape on the moors to show me just how trivial my fears of flying in command again had been. But where relief from guilt was concerned – condonation even –, that was a totally different kettle of fish. Or can of worms, rather. For delving that deeply would bring her perilously close to the substance of the dream. Desperately I had sought out an unhurried tone.

'No, nothing like that, I'm afraid. But I suppose I really didn't allow for the stress I've been under. Though you've told me often enough …'

Olive branch thus limply wagged, I had paused, and waited. Hoping to outwait her, and then pass on to the safer subject of moving in together and all that entailed. But I had been uncomfortably aware that Helen could outwait for England. Or, certainly for Girton.

'My demons? No, I can't say anything's changed there. Not a bit. And I'm not surprised, for I still think I've called it right on that score.'

Again, I had waited. Until again, I had dared wait no longer.

'Helen, I'm sorry,' I had forced a chuckle that, even to me, had sounded more like a choke, 'we'll have to continue to differ there. But, demons, gremlins, if I find I'm stuck with them, like what it seems, I'll just have to keep them grounded: infect 'em with headcolds, then off-load the little buggers! A captain's bounden dooty to their ear drums. But as far as getting the job done, safely, and responsibly, I just know I can handle it now.'

Again I had paused. And again there had been silence. But for her breathing.

'And that's not speculation. The proof will be in the next few flights. Anything that gets in the way of my actual operation will show up long before I'm checked out.'

'We'll see.'

She had still been far from satisfied. I could tell that. There had been yet another pause. Clearly she was mulling all this over, I sensed, even more deeply than normal. A cessation was all I could hope for. She was never actually going to let it drop. Not as long as she suspected that I was holding out on her. Although where her tactics left off and her strategy began – or vice versa – would keep me guessing, I liked to hope, for many a year to come.

But clearly she had reached some conclusion. For when she had spoken again, just a moment later, her voice had deepened, embodying for the first time since the call had begun that joyous quality, that enriching warmth – an intimate embrace in its own right – that I knew so well and loved so much.

'That woman you don't want to let go. She isn't going anywhere. Even if it means letting you keep that ugly little flat of yours.' Then, role player par excellence that she is, she had dropped into an uncharacteristic, and totally unconvincing,

wheedling. 'But of course, if you insist on getting shot of it ...'
Then she had laughed, throatily. And switching to the hoyden
she delights at times to be, arousingly. 'So how soon can you
shift yourself into my bed; lock, stock, barrel, burdened-soul an'
all?'

We had kept the call going for another ten minutes.
'Just now, you said "language". – Berk? Innocuous, surely?'
'Berkeley Hunt. Didn't they teach you anything but
Shakespeare at Girton?'
Shortly after which the exchanges had become too disjointed to
be usefully recorded, each of us finishing more than half the
other's utterings. And besides, although I have an Englishman's
reserve, Helen, though no less English, is in comparison very
highly charged – in a warm, womanly sort of way. Accordingly I
had left the kiosk heated, and with a very silly smile.

Before going public again, I had been obliged to wait until
what was, in truth, a leer, to efface itself. And, of course, the
other thing. Accordingly I had dawdled for a space, ostensibly
poring over the stylish repository of the former 'Sheffield Joint
Omnibuses Bus Stops'. Only then returning to the bar,
respectable, and with sober mien once more.

But what I had borne with me, gleefully clasping it close, was
the knowledge that I had still not burdened Helen with the dream.
That, I had been determined, would remain my affliction alone.
For I had yet again reached the conclusion, only even more
certainly this time than ever before, that I never would, in all my
days, find a power to grant me the relief from guilt I craved. But
– I had mentally ground my teeth – mind over matter, whatever it
took, I would make absolutely certain sure that my affliction
never, ever posed a threat to Helen, weigh upon me as it might.

Back in the warmth, I had decided upon just one more pint. To be followed by a hot bath, and then bed, to check out the restorative value of the good night's rest recommended by the doctor. The next morning would be time enough to decide whether to walk back across the tops to either Hope or Edale, or to play it safe and hitch lifts to Sheffield's Interchange right away. For some while by then I had been having trouble keeping my arguably over-tested eyes open, and although I had expected to enjoy this second pint I had been truly glad to see the bottom of the glass.

I had nodded goodnight to the barman, but he had been busy at the shelves. Except for the old boy, who – toilet visits aside – seemed to be a fixture, there had only been two other customers in evidence, both residents, I had gathered. Grinning an acknowledgement – one of them might well provide me with an initial lift next day, if needed –, I had turned into the lobby, but then, on a whim, had made my way out onto the porch to stand for a moment or two peering towards the opaqueness that masked Seal Edge, and Kinder. I had rubbed at my chin, feeling the stubble. Had it not been for Jack's guidance I would almost certainly have been spending the night up there. And again I had been swept by a surge of remorse for my lack of sensitivity. Red on blue? If that really had been what the other fellow had called out it still meant nothing whatsoever to me. But that Jack had found it hurtful had been so obvious. Yet still I …

I had turned – and started violently. Proof positive of just how tired I was. I had not heard the door open, but I found that the old chap from the bar had taken up his position at my shoulder.

'Where did they find you?' he had asked without preamble. His voice had been gruff, matter-of-fact, and although he never once intoned 'm'duck' veined through with deepest Derbyshire. Not for a second had it occurred to me to ask who 'they' were.

'It was a case of I found them,' I had said, 'thanks to their fire.'

By then he had been gazing, just I had been, up towards the tops. The silence had lengthened, but when I had made another move to turn for the door, he had checked me, his eyes glittering in the lamplight. 'Where?'

'Not all that far from the head of Fairbrook Clough. Not towards the Downfall, more to the left.' I had paused, acutely aware that I could offer no more accurate a location. 'Where were they supposed to be?'

He had merely gazed on. But by that time the night chill had been beginning to bite. And after a moment I had again begun to edge around him.

'Where the need is,' he had said cryptically then, checking me once more, and this time stretching out a liver-spotted hand. A veritable Ancient Mariner, this, complete to the 'grey beard and glittering eye'!

I had grunted. And had then seen that his protuberant knuckles had been bunched around a yellow, state-of-the-art Post-it. 'Have a word,' he had growled. And had shuffled away across the car park.

He had left his car conveniently parallel parked, facing the drive. Maybe to avoid plunging down the bank into the road. The plight of one unfortunate, according to a photo I remembered from my last visit. The starter motor had whirred weakly, but had caught at the second attempt. If I knew anything about cars I would have said that the tappets needed something doing to them. Or something. He had delayed swinging the wheel in order to pass as close to the porch as possible, then slowed. The window had been wound down.

'What do you fly?' he had called.

I had frowned, wondering where on earth that had come from. Evidently from something he had heard me say to the doctor. Although I had taken great pains to avoid any disclosure that might link me to aviation; anything that might have put it into the Service doctor's mind that my semi-concussion ought to be brought to the notice of the civil-aviation medics. Having so nearly lost my medical category I wanted as little truck as possible with that crew. Keeping quiet about the dream had been no picnic. But nor had persuading their therapists that having a brace of poorly-stiff limbs did not make me mentally challenged. Now I had started butting rocks!

As always such reflections warmed me to the relative miracles Helen had wrought once she had come on the scene. Unofficial miracles though they had to be. And grounds enough, I still suspected, to have me hung, drawn, and sectioned, and Helen burnt at the stake. But in truth, my barrack-room-lawyer vapourings aside, the establishment had done me proud. Only the relief to get that medical licence signed up! Off the hook! Or at least, as always in aviation, for the next six months. One wonders what the mafia and the Catholic Church combined could do with half the aviation-medics' power!

What do I fly, the old chap had asked.
'Medium-range transports, mainly.'
'RAF?'
'Civil, nowadays.'
He had said nothing more. Simply wound up the window and driven off, turning in the direction of Glossop and leaving me standing there, a little bemused, more than a little drained, and with a yellow Post-it in my hand.

Holding it to the light I had made out a name and address, a telephone number, and surprising me yet further, an e-mail address. But apart from finding it slightly unreal that the location should be Huddersfield, nothing had really registered. Dully, I had pulled out my wallet. To find the Post-it's sticky edge so adamantly set against entering any of the compartments that in the end I had stowed the wallet again and shoved the slip deep into a pocket. Then I had yawned. All in all it had been a very long, and a very un-straightforward day.

If anything the hot bath had acted as a stimulant, so that shattered as I had been I had found it surprisingly difficult to get off to sleep. There had still been loose ends to tie up; long ones, some of them. But moving in with Helen had no longer been one of them. My last waking awareness, therefore, should have seen my mind luxuriating on that. Instead I had found myself wrestling with a feeling of chagrin because I had not tried my Ancient-Mariner with the 'Red on Blue' enigma. Knowing the hills, he undoubtedly knew about sheep. But as I had drifted off I had concluded that I might just as well have recited the whole of Coleridge's saga to him, for all the good it would have done me.

Chapter Fifteen

The sleep that had finally claimed me had been deeply satisfying. It had not, however, been proof against some very late arrivals banging their door then dropping boot after boot from ceiling height. And with the immediate edge taken off my tiredness I had accepted with fatalistic certainty that it would now be another night of anguish; that, no longer drugged with tiredness, I would once more dream the dream.

Indeed in what I had pre-judged to be a futile attempt at pre-empting such a visitation – futile, because the stratagem had always failed me in the past –, I had run it through myself. As in a private screening. As the psychiatrists, and Helen, would have had me do; had I ever let them know of it. Recalling each detail was no bother. There had been so many hideous visitations that I could have scripted it verbatim. It never varied.

I am poised in mid-aisle, facing the tail, forward of the rear-mounted engines, aft of the swept-back wings. Passengers fill the last half-dozen rows. Their faces are featureless, mere blanks of visages. Except for eyes. Large and soulful eyes. Long-lashed, and languorous. Calm, untroubled, trusting. Beyond them, likewise void of other facial features, my two aft-cabin-staff are strapped into their seats, ready for landing.

The light-aircraft's right wing tip appears through the cabin wall to my left, sharp as a shark's fin, improbably, even in the dream world, retaining its own integrity as it cleaves through the seat-backs and decapitates my seven, abruptly eyeless, passengers on that side. With one accord all fourteen pairs of eyes across the gangway turn. Coolly, and untroubled still, they regard the gaping fuselage wall. They watch impassively as the equally faceless occupants of the impacting aircraft ineffectually raise warding-off arms as their machine rips off my starboard engine. With unfazed equanimity the fourteen watch on as paraffin jets from the ruptured fuel lines, bursts into flames, and is lashed rearwards by the airstream.

Beneath my feet my already descending aircraft, as of its own volition, banks over and ever more steeply noses earthwards. But this brings no sense of menace. Only utterly unreal silence. A silence somehow punctuated by a voice. Just one voice, high-keyed, panic-frayed, unintelligible, but unceasing. And only too recognisable as my own.

The wheels make contact with the runway. And I hear myself shriek that fateful order, 'Reverse thrust!' So that instantly the remaining engine's braking airflow surges around from both above and below the fuselage to snatch back the flames and blow-torch them directly into the rear cabin.

But more immediately every last eye has turned to mine. Fourteen plaintive Gollums. Fourteen sorrowful ETs. Each eye is placid. Calm, and trusting still. Then unease appears. And deepens. Becomes worry. Then concern. Then all are whitely frenzied, and sick with trust betrayed, with sudden, frantic terror. Now each wells blood to course down bones where cheeks should be. I stand accused. Arraigned. Condemned. The unspoken sentence sears.

'We, collectively, trusted you! We, collectively, damn your soul!'

Each eye fixates. Bereft of tears, each liquefies, but does not moisten. And so dissolves. And in a moment – a moment with eternity enclosed – the whole, now-horrid load parts company at my feet to leave me poised above a speeding, tarmac-floored abyss.

And then time compresses, and I am in that distant hangar, standing before those torpid body bags. I have no need to count them. Twenty-three in total. Fourteen to my own account. I would like to turn away. But paralysis, with bony, gripping talons, turns each limb to stone. When my silent, incoherent scream, awakens me.

'Limb dysfunction, fundamentally psychosomatic.'

The medical doctors had eventually upped sticks. After that, with the psychiatrists, and with my livelihood at stake, I had effectively stuck to the equivalent of number, rank, name, and date of birth for as long as it took. And my reticence, and subsequently, Helen's expertise, had finally paid off.

But it had not been the dream alone I had held back on. For the pragmatic defensive tactic I had developed to employ against it had also remained my secret. And it had worked. For although almost nightly I would start into wakefulness shocked, rigid with terror, and soaked in sweat, the tactic had acted so swiftly that not even Helen, on two occasions actually under the same duvet, had been aware of my distress.

My defence had been to rationalise that I could not possibly have witnessed events at the rear while strapped into my captain's left-hand seat at the sharp end. From which it followed that the nocturnally played-out sequence was not reality, but merely the product of my stunned mind. Nothing but a distorted amalgam of voice tapes, witness statements, expert deliberations, and a spectator's video. A mixture blended by my imagination, itself unnaturally inflamed by what had happened to my charges. The defensive remedy had been successful as a tactic. But not as a strategy. And only as a palliative. For there was no cure.

Notwithstanding the proven success of my method, however, I have – or had, until this evening, at least – found neither tactic nor strategy to help me reason out why the dream saw fit to change the way it did that night. For when I had eventually fallen off again what I had dreamed was no longer nightmarish but rationality personified.

I am in the aircraft once again. Only this time, significantly, I am not in the rear cabin, but on the flight-deck, and in my accustomed seat. My first officer is once more flying the leg, the cabin staff have reported the cabin secure, landing clearance has been received, the gear is down, and the runway is in sight through scattered cloud. The sudden pop-up appearance of the light aircraft has taken even air traffic control unawares, so that all we know is that an impact, otherwise bearing vague similarities to wake turbulence, has rolled us off the centre line.

Having expected my colleague to make an instant correction I shoot a concerned look across at him as the aircraft continues to heel over, its descent rate increasing. But now the verbal exchanges that follow are those I know so well from countless playbacks of the cockpit voice-recorder. As always, I strain to detect some hint of the panic that, at the time, had fought like a wild thing within me for domination. Ever expecting to hear it, yet never managing to do so.

'I can't hold it, Mark!' my first officer cries. Bringing my seemingly collected, 'I have control,' and his conditioned response the relinquishment called for, the procedurally-formal, 'You have control, sir.'

Just as it had been then, it is gut feeling once again. I have no idea what has happened at the rear. All I know is that the aircraft is rolling and its descent steepening ever further. I slam shut both power levers, and feel again the load on my left leg as I lock the knee to give the full rudder demanded by the abnormal yaw. I see my right forearm cord with strain as, at the same time, I wind over the yoke to check the downgoing wing.

'Round again, to sort things out?' my colleague grits.

'No.' My return is emphatic.

And again I hear his immediate, and very proper protest, 'We're too high now.' And even my affirmative grunt. For we are indeed.

'Advise the tower.'

There is no hesitation, but he is clearly a child of his time, and his, 'Mayday. Possible bomb blast. Landing,' is succinctness itself. Even so my voice on the passenger-address blots out his last word.

'Ladies and gentlemen. Stay calm. Brace for a firm landing. Cabin staff, use all exits.'

All exits. I know that the wind is light, and blowing straight down the runway. In the event of a fire on touchdown then, evacuating passengers will be no more menaced by wind-blown flames on one side than the other. I cannot know that the tail is already ablaze and that the fire-warning circuits have been ripped away.

The controls are now slack, now heavy, the load altering with every instant. So once more it is gut feeling alone that insists that I place no extra strain on the structure by unduly rounding out before touchdown.

I snatch the chance to re-examine my colleague's eminently sensible suggestion of buying time to sort things out by climbing away then coolly working through what might have happened. Only here again instinct – certainly not reason –, operates.

'The sooner we get this heap on the ground and stopped, the better.'

Touchdown, and far harder than I had envisaged, far too fast, and far too far down the runway for comfort. Now I simply have to get the aircraft stopped! The spoilers, disrupting the lift across the wings, have already deployed but will be losing their effectiveness with every yard that passes. The toe-brakes are powerful. But not powerful enough. Not at this speed. They can be brought into play later. Now it is engine-power braking I need.

'Reverse thrust,' I order. The normal primary-braking method after touchdown.

With my left leg trembling with strain and my right arm locked it is my first officer who actuates the levers. Only there is an uncharacteristically muted roar on this occasion as, unexpectedly, just one engine responds. Just one! And the aircraft swings violently. Then again I hear what comes to us as a mere muffled thump as the rear end blows away.

'On the brakes – you too,' I order.

And then just moments later, with none of the braking aids having any appreciable effect, and as the open space ahead continues to diminish with now-alarming rapidity, I order, 'Retract the gear.'

And once again, just as on the tape, I hear the screeching as the wheels fold up and the belly subsides onto the tarmac. My imperative on the passenger address is clear too.

'Evacuate, evacuate, all exits.'

Once again the first officer levers himself through his side window, then I take to my own escape rope.

The fire vehicles are already roaring into place. With the rear evacuation slide gone I am helping passengers down the crumpled port wing instead, eyeing cabin staff shepherding others from the front slide, and dully regarding the whole rear fuselage, a lurid inferno, some hundreds of yards back along the debris-littered runway.

Only now does the time sequence telescope, and detail go awry. For, seemingly without opposition – whereas at the time all efforts were directed towards dissuading me –, I am in the hangar, and before me are the so-silent body bags. Twenty-three of them. And in particular, though indistinguishable from the others, the fourteen that need not have been there but for my 'reverse thrust' order.

And just as it had been then, it is as I turn away that I realise that neither my overstrained right arm nor my locked left leg are functioning as they should.

Chapter Sixteen

I had awoken, still in the small hours, but to discover, for the first time in a countless succession of months, a calm mind. To discover too, with no small degree of wonderment, that rationality had finally returned; or at least, rationality in considerable measure. I would gladly have given a fortune had that return to normality enabled me to discuss the reason for the change of dream with Helen. But I had never been one for too-closely examining gift horses.

I had been only too grateful, therefore, to find that, for the first time since the accident, I had been able to give due weight to the hours the enquiry had spent in dissecting and assessing what I could still only see as seat-of-the-pants reactions. I had long since accepted that they had judged the whole well handled. As I had been forced to accept the laurels heaped upon me by both company and the Civil Aviation Authority; more surprisingly by survivors and even the relatives of some of those who had died; and far less surprisingly, by the hero-seeking media.

This general consensus of approval then, I had found myself able to accept. But only just. Now, however, I had awoken to find that I no longer harboured even the most fleeting of doubts regarding the professional correctness of my decision making. That in itself had been a benediction; a more merciful relief than I could ever have envisaged. Yet circumstances had still prevented me from making a clean breast of things to Helen.

For the change of dream had not diminished by one whit the overburdening guilt that had ridden me for so long! I had realised this in that self-same instant of awakening. True, the nightmare dream had signally changed. But the body bags remained.

I had, of course, immediately recognised the new dream sequence as a significant onward move. But also as one that went nowhere near far enough. It had certainly not been the development to bring the soul-soothing quietude Helen had predicted.

Nor did it yet weigh with me, as a move towards relieving my guilt, that Everyman and his dog had endorsed my actions. Similarly I could still derive not the least comfort from the video, submitted by an airport spectator, which had been used in an effort to convince me that the fire would have engulfed the whole aircraft had I not, effectively, blown away the rear section. For persuasive as such arguments derived from film and flight recorder had been, it could only be speculation that all one hundred and forty-five passengers and crew might otherwise have died. The insurmountable fact being that, but for my order to reverse the thrust, twelve passengers and two crew members might not have died.

At that stage, still being, as I now suspect, both physically and mentally drained, I had fallen off into an easy sleep. Certainly the next few hours, and yet another hot bath on finally arising, had turned me from the previous night's wet rag into something more like my normal self. Just the same I had decided to play it safe, and instead of heading back into the hills I had indeed cadged a lift from one of the residents from the night before. He had been going to Grimsby, it had transpired, and had driven me to Sheffield railway station itself. And my luck had held there, for a timely train, running only twenty minutes late, had eventually deposited me in Derby.

That there had followed a four-hour wait in the Accident and Emergency department had been frustrating, if not entirely unanticipated. Yet, had my mobile phone been working, it would have been more fraught still, with me on edge in case Helen phoned, and in her devious way discovered where I was. But the phone had remained dodo dead, rendering me incommunicado. And after a passage of time a succession of white gowns with blunt fingers and bright lights had arrived, ultimately deciding that none of my cogs had been knocked out of kilter by my cerebellum-stunning performance of the day before.

So it had been that by three in the afternoon I had walked out past the fag-dragging ambulance crews, a free spirit, in supposedly sound mind, with approved hearing response, certified-A1 sight – subject to spectacles, as my Air Transport Pilot's Licence specifies. And weak with relief that the medics had not discovered my association with aviation and insisted upon directing me to the Ministry for further checks. I had also acquired a brand-new plaster for my shin. Not forgetting something else I had required some considerable time before that, namely a respect for the Kinder Plateau such as I had never before conceived.

But what had been foremost in my mind had been to hold Helen in my arms once more, and so assuage the need for her presence engendered by the last couple of not too humdrum days.

In the period since, the gash on my leg has healed. And six days after my moorland foray, with my final refresher-training flight behind me, and having completed my first commercial flight in command for over two years, I had returned to the flat to find a smiling Helen, poised expectantly. I had swept her close.

'All signed up! That was this morning. Real passengers this afternoon. And still no problems!'

Some considerable time later, when I had released her and she had caught her breath, she had asked, 'No misgivings?'

I had shaken my head. Since my initial refresher-training flight there had been no recurrence of the qualms that had so bothered me on that occasion. Meaning that what had occurred had been an attack of the jitters, exacerbated by the tragedy, of course, but made infinitely worse by the corrosive nature of the dream. More, to date there has been no repetition of the new dream either.

Such reasoning being tendered with fingers firmly crossed, however, no landing being complete until the wheels are chocked.

Just the same, as dilemmas go, so dilemmas come. For although, especially after that first commercial flight, I had burned to ask Helen to rule on the dream having become so unexpectedly benign, I had dared not broach the subject. Nothing had changed where that had been concerned. And to broach that subject would still have meant comparing the new dream with the still-undisclosed old one.

'*Become* benign,' she would have asked at once, 'become from what?'

And then my fat would have been well and truly in the fire.

So asking her to rule on the dream had never been an option. Not without I weakened so far as to throw over all my resolutions in order to gain the relief of spilling out my soul. And that I simply could not do. And never would, as I had long resolved. At the very least to do so would mean my giving Helen chapter and verse of that traumatic evening on the moors, thereby burdening her with how nearly I had come to giving up. No. Nothing had changed in that department. My 'close pent up guilts', and all that sailed in them must continue to be a most necessary case of 'what the eye doesn't see'. They were dormant at the moment. But they would be back. For what should lift them from my conscience?

'Misgivings? Sorry, Helen,' I had become acutely aware that she must have been regarding me for far longer than a normal conversational period allowed. 'I'd wandered off a bit. Misgivings? Nope. Nary a one.'

'Guilty feelings?'

I had smiled down at her. 'I must be less pragmatic than I'd thought. They've simply sorted themselves out. Just qualms, after all. You were right. Again.'

Characteristically she had ignored that sop, maintaining instead her intense regard, her eyes unwavering on mine. At length, a tooth dimpling her lower lip, she had frowned.

'Captain Johnston, sir, the reason I got through to you where the Ministry's people couldn't, was that you relaxed with me. It wasn't that I broke down barriers, it was you that let them down. But never altogether. And you're still protecting the core.'

And then she had dropped her eyes. And the subject. And had kept her own counsel. In what amounted to a truce. Although that would obtain, I had known full well, only so long as she decided it should.

Days before that, however, having shown in an unmistakable fashion her delight at my decision 'to finally commit', as she had put it, Helen had urged me to organise ending the lease on my flat. She had wanted it done at once but had been forced to concede that the financial penalty would have been too great. It had been settled finally that I would soldier out the lease then formally move in with her at the beginning of January.

During my off-duty periods in the interim, and when Helen has been otherwise engaged, I have, on two occasions, headed off to Kinder again. Both somewhat enigmatic visits. But made equipped with serviceable head torch, fully-charged mobile phone, disinfectant swabs, a manufacturer's-specification cord securing my rather costly backlit Silva compass, and a spare compass stowed safely in my rucksack. Never forgetting the hand-held satellite navigator Helen has insisted on my learning how to use!

Chapter Seventeen

And already it is Christmas Eve! But with Helen, according to her in-flight e-mail, pointing in this direction but presently suspended somewhere over the North Atlantic, I had found myself at an anticipated loose end. So it was that I had decided to make the phone-call tonight.

Or, pondering that … Did I decide? And if I did, had it truly been my decision? For until I had walked across the room to retrieve the old fellow's Post-it I had not even considered 'having a word' since that encounter at the Snake Inn. Nor would I normally disturb anyone with a phone call that late in the evening, let alone a total stranger, and least of all on such a special evening. Indeed I had mapped out a pick-and-choose television schedule, I had Helen's mince pies and my decanter to hand, and I had been about to indulge in my first port of the festive season when the compulsion had come upon me.

In truth, the Post-it had not even come to light again until it had been through the wash in my Gore-tex. And by that time the directions had been only partly decipherable. Nonetheless, I had randomly tucked it between two books. Indeed thinking back I recall having idly wondered at the ease with which, just minutes since, I had located it on bookshelves which normally delight in hiding any book I search for.

The e-mail address had vanished altogether along with most of the postal directions. But I had been able to make out the phone number itself. And although the Huddersfield area code was corrupt, directory enquiries had put me right.

Sensible then, of the special significance of the festive season, putting myself in the place of anyone getting a cold call, and not all that certain that I had deciphered the main number correctly anyway, I found myself fighting off a sudden distaste for making the call at all. Perhaps because of that, when the phone was answered I was caught on the hop. So much so that I failed to take in the man's name.

'Hello, Mr – er … I'm afraid I don't know your name, it washed off –'

I stopped, and collected myself. Starting again, I apologised for intruding on Christmas Eve, introduced myself, and assimilated, this time, that he was Henry Cotterell.

'A while back,' I told him, diving straight in now that I was committed, 'a chap in a pub, an estate manager, possibly – I didn't get his name –, said to call you.'

'Yes?' said Henry Cotterell non-committally. He was evidently as wary as I am of sales pitches made at any time of day and paraded under any guise.

So far I had gathered from his voice that Mr Cotterell was not in the first flush of youth, that he was precisely-, rather than well-spoken, that he did not suffer fools over gladly; and that he was waiting, very politely, but only too evidently waiting just the same, to get back to the television programme I could hear in the background.

'He gave me a Post-it note, sir. But I inadvertently put it through the washer.'

'The washer …!' He made it sound so much like Lady Bracknell's, 'A handbag!' that had I had the forethought to key in 141 before making the call I might well have put the phone down right then.

Now, a scant half hour later, at most, perhaps I wish I had done.

'What it was,' I tried again, 'I'd been walking up on Kinder – '

There was no detectable reaction. But I knew on the instant, certainly before he spoke, that his attitude had changed completely.

'Wait –, please!' His voice, vibrantly alert suddenly, became muffled, and I heard him talk to someone else in the room; clearly unaware of the inefficacy of palming a modern phone. There was a pause, then I heard another instrument lifted, and a click as the first one was put down. When he came on again there was a barely-suppressed excitement in his voice – and perhaps just a hint of something more, something akin to apprehension.

'Look, I'm sorry about that, Mr –' Clearly he was no better at retaining names than I was. I reminded him. 'Yes, of course, Mr Johnston. But it'll be better if I take this in my study here. Quieter.' He paused, and I heard him blow his nose. 'Apologies, headcold …'

It was my turn now to wait while he collected himself. Which took only seconds. When he spoke again, he had become calm, matter-of-fact.

'Do you fly?'

The question came rocketing out of the blue. 'That's pretty well what he asked,' I said finally, 'the old chap –'

'And?'

'I'm an airline captain.' And then, remembering, 'I was RAF before that.'

'You said you were on Kinder. In trouble, obviously.'

It was not a question exactly, but I decided to go with the swim. 'I was walking, slipped down, got concussed, and went astray, that's all.'

He paused. Then said musingly, 'So there had to be something else …' I waited through a more protracted pause. 'Can you tell me about it?'

Gathering my thoughts, and trying to avoid too much detail, I described the fall, my dazed wanderings, and the way sighting the fire had put new heart into me; stressing rather more, my profound relief at finding that the steady burn had obliged the estate workers to stay on.

The recital took several minutes, during which time the only sound from the end of the line was the occasional nose-blow. Yet I was never in doubt that I had his full attention. I stopped at that point. And for a full minute, it must have been, we were both of us sitting in silence.

Then I heard him clear his throat. And the sound of his chair, shifting. 'They were by a pool.'

I frowned at the instrument. That was a detail I had not bothered with. 'That's right.'

'A pool larger than any you'd seen before, on Kinder.' His voice no longer held that earlier buzz of excitement. Now there was a fateful quality about it. 'A pool edged about with rushes.'

'Rushes, yes; and the largest-ever pool.'

'And the fire?'

I cast my mind back. 'It was lapping the edge of the water.' I saw again the iridescent shimmering upon the surface, so reminiscent of petrol. 'It couldn't have burned much longer. – But the old chap, you know who he was then?'

'*Them*, tell me about –, them.'

I recognised, on the instant, that this was to be a one-sided exchange that admitted to no accepted rule of first give, then take. It was a technique I had, until now, associated only with television barristers, and certain females. With Helen in the van. And yet, whereas in the past this had often riled, nothing seemed more natural, or more acceptable, than Henry Cotterell's total domination of the conversation; and further, his abstraction from it into realms with which he alone was familiar.

'There were seven of them,' he led.

Again, I frowned. 'That's right.– I think they were the old chap's gang. Estate workers. Shepherds, possibly. But he would have made taciturn sound chatty. – You seem to know all about them, though.' Suddenly it came to me that I might be unnecessarily exercising too much restraint. 'So, why did he suggest I call you? Why your interest?'

For a long moment I thought he would ignore this altogether, would sidetrack me, or simply not answer. But I was wrong. In part.

'He was a shepherd once. When he was younger.' For the first time, he laughed. Just a brief bark. Yet even then a certain wryness came through. 'When we were both younger.'

Again there was a pause. But there were questions pressing to be asked. The first had to be, 'What the hell's it got to do with me?' And there were several more. 'Why am I phoning you?' 'So, he was a shepherd, now he's an estate manager, so what?' Not least, 'What's my being a flyer got to do with anything?' And there were others, jostling for precedence. Only, much to my own surprise, I asked none of them.

He cleared his throat again. 'In 1944, when I first met him – his name is Slack, by the way, Andrew Slack – I was twenty. And on Lancs – Lancasters.'

The situation was suddenly reversed. He had my interest now. 'On ops?'

'I had done a full tour by then.' He paused. 'Me –, and of course, the Skipper, and the lads.'

I whistled my respect. 'At twenty!– You say "the Skipper", so you were his –?'

'Navigator.'

'Not many crews survived a full tour.' I even knew the statistics. Only one in three aircrew could expect to finish a tour of thirty bomber operations.

'In the end, I finished a second tour.'

'*Finished* a second!'

That represented far longer odds. Almost infinitely longer. Again, I knew that of all the aircrew who passed through Bomber Command – over 125,000 of them in the course of the war, and none of them pressed men –, less than 7,000 even volunteered for a second tour, let alone survived it. As for those who flew on beyond a second tour – men like Guy Gibson and Leonard Cheshire, with Cheshire completing over one hundred bomber operations – they were stars isolated in their own firmament.

'And your captain, and crew, the same?'

The answer was a long time coming. 'No.'

I mulled that over, trying to fit things together. 'So you met the old man – Slack – at that time?'

'Nobody could tell me what had happened. Or nothing that made sense. To my mind everything pointed to Kinder. I was due leave. I based myself at the Snake Inn – I imagine that's where Andrew made contact with you?'

I frowned somewhat at that, but mouthed, 'That's right.'

'Then I started my own search. Caught up with Andrew. He'd reported an explosion. And he helped. As he's been helping ever since.'

'Like giving me your number?'

'That's the way of it.' He paused. 'Despite the bang you took, you seem to have remained pretty well compos mentis throughout. Certainly you're by far my best hope yet.' A note of puzzlement became detectable. 'You fell, and hurt your head, you say. Even so, there must be something else about you …'

I had no idea what that 'something else' could be; but if I were the best of anything, all that came to mind was that I was far from the brightest. I was a forlorn hope, at most, whatever he thought I had to offer. And at the moment I could not even guess at the nature of the bee he had in his bonnet.

Chapter Eighteen

'I must admit, Mr Cotterell,' I told him apologetically, 'that I really can't fathom where you're going here. But,' I hastened to reassure him, 'I can see you've to go about things in your own way, so if you'll bear with my being slow on the uptake, then I'll just bide my time.'

I heard him grunt with satisfaction. And relief, I fancied. 'As I said,' he reiterated, 'You're my best hope yet.'

I pondered that. The comparative, not the superlative. 'That pre-supposes others.'

'Harold Gretorix, from Edale, sent me four. He was, you might say, Andrew's counterpart on the far side of Kinder. But he died five years ago.' I heard him turn the pages of a book. 'Four from Harold, then. Plus two he directed to me twelve years ago who never made contact. And six from Andrew – seven now, with you. Thirteen all together.' I said nothing. But clearly he was not waiting for a comment. 'At Mermaid's Pool, Kinder Low, Druid's Stone, Jaggers Clough ... Now Fair Brook ...' His voice tailed off. But after a while he went on, musingly again, 'There are bound to have been others. But even that's not a bad return.' He paused once more, before adding, in a mutter barely audible to me, 'Disappointing, just the same. For none of them, I've always suspected, have been quite what was wanted ... So perhaps you ...'

It suddenly struck me that he was searching for reinforcement of some premise – some near obsession, I was beginning to think – that he had maintained, by the sound of it, for almost sixty years. Searching? Perhaps pleading for it was closer to the mark. And yet I could offer him nothing. It was his version of my own vain search for some dispeller of guilt. I said tentatively, 'But with my deafness, I've been able to tell you very little. What about the others?'

'Even less. Almost all were in much worse condition than you. Some physically. All were very low psychologically – the state of mind's evidently the key to the way it works.' He paused, then with that note of puzzlement again, muttered, 'But, not the whole key …'

'There's a scheme, you feel. An operating mechanism.' I tried him with humour. 'A "suitable system of levers", you'd say?'

The reference, common to both of us from ground-school classrooms, raised a dry chuckle. 'Not all were regular aircrew. One was a flying-club pupil.'

'But no one unassociated with flying?'

'It seems not. Hard, eh! Ignoring others in trouble. On the other hand, aviating, per se, clearly isn't the fundamental operator.'

To hell with this, I decided. For minutes on end now I had been feeling distinctly uneasy. Why, I could not fathom. Although I put it down to being uncertain about what was going on here. And I have never been happy with uncertainty.

'Tell me what this is about,' I demanded.

He did not reply for so long that I feared I might have pressured him too hard, that he might simply terminate the conversation and put down the phone. From what I could gather he now had nearly all he could have wanted from me, whatever that had been. For there was nothing relevant I had not told him. My own mind, however, inherently sceptical that anything in nature should be held unexplainable, was now filled with the most disquieting apprehensions.

At length I heard him cough, then clear his nose. Even then the ensuing silence lasted so long that when he began to speak again it came as something of a shock. And now his voice was clear, direct, and confident. And as fluid and articulate, without pause or deviation, as if he were reciting from a script that Time had written on his heart. Which, as I now suppose, is exactly what he was doing.

'At that stage of the war, the number of bomber operations that counted as a tour had stabilised at thirty. We'd come together as a crew back in OTU – you'll know?'

He paused, and I grunted my familiarity: Operational Training Unit; essentially where newly-qualified aircrew were melded into operational bomber crews; Operational Conversion Unit by my day.

'And not one of us had missed an op to date. This was our thirtieth. After it we were tour-ex. We had a celebration booked, in Lincoln. Then we were off on ten days' leave. But we weren't finished. We'd volunteered, and been accepted, the whole crew, onto Pathfinder Force.'

He paused, evidently to address his tissue once again.

'This op, the thirtieth, was to Bremen, to the Ruhr. Never a piece of cake. And over the target half the bomb load hung up. Then, on the way back, a night fighter did for the starboard outer engine, so that the prop windmilled, and couldn't be feathered.'

I grunted. As the propeller blades on that engine could not be turned into the wind to minimise the drag they would have caused an enormous pull to the right.

'Jerry's bursts also seriously wounded our wireless op, Reg Pearce, in the leg. They did other damage too, smashing the compass repeater, and worse, the artificial horizon. But they also partially jammed the ailerons; which meant that the Skipper had even more difficulty in keeping the kite's right wing up. Then again, over and above losing some lateral control, he'd been left with a rudder problem.'

So, I supplied silently, in order to keep the aircraft going in the right direction his pilot would have had to maintain a hefty manual control load the whole way back; not just for minutes, as

I had, but for hours on end! And with fellow feeling I could picture his limbs beginning to quiver under the protracted strain! Yet relax the pressure for an instant on either rudder or wheel and the nose would skid sideways under the braking effect of the windmilling propeller. The effect of which would be to roll the aircraft onto its back, so that within moments the whole concern would be on a downward spiral to oblivion.

The picture had come to me so vividly – recalling how my aircraft too had been set to spiral into the ground – that it took a moment to realise that Cotterell had paused. Afraid that he would think I had lost interest I prompted hastily, 'But you made it back to base?'

Again the silence dragged on. Then he blew his nose once more.

'As you well know, the prevailing wind over the UK is westerly. Only that night it was one of those unusually strong easterlies, low down. Rushing in from Russia, we always said. Apart from that the weather wasn't bad, ten-tenths cloud at a good eight hundred feet above the aerodrome. As for hills, coming from Germany there was nothing but the Wolds to keep in mind, and they can't be more than four hundred feet high.'

He paused, to give a large sniff.

'Eventually the Skipper called that he was approaching the overhead, still in thick cloud. He told the tower that he intended to head out for the sea again while letting down to 2,000 feet. After which he'd turn back towards the field, and continue descending on a westerly heading until he broke cloud.'

Another sniff.

'They warned him of the strong wind, so he told them he'd fly towards the sea – ploughing into the headwind – that much longer, in order to compensate.'

His voice stopped abruptly. And I took advantage of the pause to ease my arm muscle and change the telephone to the other hand – headsets suit me so much better!

While waiting for him to resume I mulled over the procedure he had described, finally nodding approval. Certainly it seemed that pretty well all eventualities had been taken into consideration. With all that control damage the critical thing would have been that turn, back towards the airfield.

I continued to wait, but the silence finally outlasted my patience. 'So that's what you did?'

Even that failed to spur him on. But just as I was about to prompt him again, he said dully, 'There were no more calls. – Every airfield to the east, every observer post, every ack-ack site, every Air-Sea Rescue launch on station, everyone was contacted –, but nothing. Then forty minutes later a report came in that what was thought to be an aircraft had exploded on high ground to the west! Forty bloody miles to the west! But from the east, from the seaward side, nothing. And later, nothing to the west either. No confirmation of the earlier report. Not a trace of wreckage.'

Being a pragmatist, my tactic against the nightmare had been to argue against the inconsistency embodied, demanding, 'How could I possibly have seen...?' In Cotterell's account too the evident dissonance rankled. I knew, if I waited, Cotterell would explain it. But with impatience driving me I was just about to press him to do so, when he cleared his throat.

'I wasn't with them, of course. I'd been stood down. I'd developed a headcold; I've always been susceptible. My ears were bunged solid. But I'd kitted-up, briefed, the lot. Only the Skipper caught on. Flatly refused to fly me. Joked that my grandchildren'd never forgive him if he burst my eardrums in the descent, and permanently deafened me.'

Again I heard him resort to his tissue – his handkerchief, whatever; he was of a linen generation, after all.

'So some other nav went along, in your place.'

He merely grunted.

'And you?'

'I'd got permission to wait in the tower; that's how I heard what the Skipper told them, over the loudspeaker. Two days later, my ears cleared, and I finished off my tour with another crew. A milk run to a French port. Then I got my leave. And began my search.'

'And that's when you met, what's his name again?'

'Andrew. Yes. I didn't know the Peak District at all. As it happened, I met him on the first day. He was certain he'd seen a flash. On Kinder. Despite the cloud. He wouldn't budge on that. Never has.'

I was puzzled. 'But why Kinder? Besides, even if they'd managed to make the remaining bombs safe there would have been debris all over the shop.'

'Not a trace.'

I thought again of the downed Lancaster, swallowed by the bog near Ely. I recalled too the privately-owned Hunter jet fighter which had buried itself so deeply into the Peakland moors that the decision had been made to leave it there – together with its owner-pilot.

'So again,' I demurred, 'why Kinder? With so much battle damage isn't it more likely that he lost control while turning back, and went into the sea? – Or that an intruder intercepted them?'

'In thick cloud? At night?'

Aware that what he must have seen as my slur on his pilot's ability had ruffled him, I chewed at my lip. And waited.

It took him a while, and obviously cost him dearly. But after a space he conceded, 'You're right, of course. Certainly they're the alternatives the court of inquiry looked at. But in the end they settled upon loss of control. Discounting altogether the Kinder sighting!'

Clearly Cotterell had never subscribed to the official findings. Clearly too the fight to set his own mind at rest had, indeed, become an obsession. All these years of being eaten up by guilt – because a headcold had prevented him from supporting his crew that night! Yet if, as seemed evident to me, the pilot had, understandably, lost control of his damaged machine in the turn and spiralled into the sea, no navigator on earth could have done anything about it. So all these years he had been caning himself for nothing.

I went to speak, but then held my tongue. I had learnt the hard way what it meant to lose an aircraft. Still more to lose passengers; and even crew members. Yet heavily though recriminations weighed upon me, my passengers had been unknown to me, and I had never as much as seen my two lost cabin staff before reporting for that day's flight. This man, on the other hand, had been bound to his crew by ties tightened in the course of nearly thirty fraught operations over enemy territory.

Eventually I could contain myself no longer. 'But what did you hope to discover? For even had you been on board you couldn't have helped them. You must know that.'

'That's never been the issue.' His voice was short.

'I see. My apologies,' I sought recourse in gnawing at my lip. 'So what exactly is it you've been after?'

'The truth. The truth about what really happened that night. For I can't accept the finding. The sheer injustice of it blackened my Skipper's reputation. And with him my crew's. And they deserved better after nearly thirty ops. The thing is, the Skipper was far too careful to make such a basic mistake, but to have ended up on Kinder, as I firmly believe they did, they had to have flown the reciprocal.'

Chapter Nineteen

I recognised at once that injustice stood on equal terms with guilt as a motivating force. After all, it had driven the American colonists to dump tea, seen off the slave trade, and underpinned the prosecution of the Second World War. Just the same, for Cotterell, still actively partisan after sixty years, to actually vocalise the possibility that his pilot might have mis-set the compass must have pained him beyond measure. The implications, after all, were chilling, and I took a moment or two to digest what flying a reciprocal course would have meant in this instance.

'*You're gnawing at your lip again.*' Hurriedly, I desisted, ever obedient these days to Helen's subconscious imprinting.

It meant that when his pilot, flying in thick cloud, at night, had thought he had been taking his crew out to sea, he had, in fact, been taking them towards Derbyshire's High Peak. Moreover, all that time the fierce wind would have been at his back, vastly increasing his speed over the ground; shades of Alice and the Queen yet again!

But it got worse, even setting aside momentarily the so-fraught business of making the reverse-direction turn. For when he eventually levelled out at what he thought was 2,000 feet over the sea he would actually have been over Kinder, and merely skimming the moor. After which his next step would have been to re-commence his descent to 800 feet in order to break cloud. Only the instant he lowered the nose to do so …

I shook my head. Violently. It was a scenario too hideous to contemplate.

True, this simplistic explanation did not account for every possibility. Besides, common sense insisted that it was far more likely that the pilot, with probably only a few hundred flying hours under his belt – the experience level of most wartime pilots –, had found the inbound turn altogether too demanding and lost control, to be swallowed by the sea. But although I had subscribed to the loss-of-control cause such a short while before, and logically still did so, suddenly I found myself unaccountably reluctant to hold to it.

At which moment, and for the first time in weeks, that once-persistent niggle stirred. That mind-tugging colour combination. Stirred. And would not be denied.

I swallowed, suddenly dry mouthed. 'Describe him to me, your pilot.'

'Right ...' Cotterell cleared his nose once again. 'He was a couple of months older than the rest of us, that's all. And the tallest by a good six inches or so. And his voice –'

'He had a moustache, the handlebar type.' I cut directly across him. Nevertheless I heard his gasp.

'Absolutely!' His excitement was unmistakable. 'He called it his "wizard-prang-weed". Aping the fighter boys. Laughing at himself, really.'

I cast my mind back. 'And a much smaller chap. Stocky lad. A real bantam –'

'Our rear gunner. Mike Barnes. "Tosh" Barnes. A tyke. A Yorkshireman. Irrepressible. I'll swear Skip's was the only authority he recognised.'

Skip!– Not Shep then, but Skip! For Skipper. I mulled that over.– The wireless operator wounded. In the leg. And one of them had never risen to his feet ... I said deliberately, 'And Jack?'

I do not claim to be overly gifted with perceptiveness, so I accept the possibility that our interchange had been carried on at more levels than I had been conscious of. But once again, even before he spoke, I sensed that all traces of enthusiasm had suddenly drained from him. His very silences had become that eloquent!

'Jack?'

'He was the one who showed me to Fair Brook. Only as we left the rest the stocky chap ribbed him. Upset him.'

'Jack Norris,' his voice came coldly down the line, 'was the replacement navigator.' His tone was devoid of emotion. 'He didn't have a regular crew.'

'You resent him having taken your place that day?'

He was in no hurry to respond. And although I was in far less of a hurry to even begin to allow my mind to properly take in what had just emerged, this time I gave him his space.

'Blame, rather than resent,' he said eventually. He did not resort to whatever nose-wipe he was using this time, but gave a loud nasal trump. 'Norris wasn't highly rated. That's why he didn't have a regular crew.'

And I remembered the crewing-up system from my earliest RAF days. You were all left in a room together. And when you emerged you were expected to have sorted yourselves out into complete crews. And the fear, among crew members of being rejected; and among pilots of being shunned ...

'In the two days before my ears cleared,' the flat voice continued, 'I hung around the squadron adjutant's office. And when he was out, I stuck my nose into Norris's personal file. It seems he'd started off as a trainee pilot. He was shaky. But they'd pushed him as far as twins – Oxfords. Then, at a very late stage of his training, he'd flown a whole series of legs on the reciprocal headings – going the wrong way on each ...'

He broke off, 'Sorry –, teaching my grandmother ...'

The unspoken protest, *Grandson*, came devoid of humour.

'The staff pilot monitoring him had given him every opportunity to twig, querying the compass course he'd set at every turning point. But Norris had just sat there. Heaven knows where they would have landed up! Taken with his general showing, it was the last straw. He was scrubbed. Then he was re-mustered to navigator. The norm for many, of course. But unlike most, he was bitter about it. As his documents reflected. And petulant. The nav school too, recommended suspension – it was all there in the record – but losses being what they were, he was passed.'

'And you believe that's what Jack Norris did that day? Gave your crew a reciprocal heading?'

'Not as such.' The admission was grudging. 'Had he said head west from overhead instead of east, everyone would have picked it up. Especially our lot, that day. Each of them had commiserated with me as they left briefing, and it was clear they weren't happy with him ...'

He checked himself, snuffled, and then went on, 'On most crews the norm was for the navigator to call the changes of heading. But on ours we'd adopted a system of our own. It had all started at OTU, on Wellingtons, when our final training trip had been an op to Cologne as part of a thousand-kite raid. Until the target I'd been beavering away at my station. With the bombs gone, I called out the heading for base. Only instead of simply acknowledging, Skip called back, 'Cotters, come and have a decko.' I'd clambered forwards to stand at his shoulder. The raid had been on for some time before we'd arrived, so that looking down I couldn't believe my eyes. Such stuff going down! Even more coming up! I understood later when some Lanc navs swore they kept their curtain drawn during ops. Anyway, at that moment we'd been coned by searchlights, and the Skipper had instantly thrown the kite onto one wing in an evasive corkscrew.

'Set the compass for me, Cotters,' he'd yelled. 'I've got my hands full here.'

And so I'd set it, spun the ring, and locked it. From then on, whenever we'd dropped our bombs, or for that matter, whenever the weather was particularly bumpy, or foggy low down, forcing him to concentrate on his instrument flying, he'd have me go up and set any major heading changes for him.'

I frowned. I had once been shown over the Lancaster maintained by the RAF's Battle of Britain Flight. Not that much room for a third body, I would have thought, what with the pilot's and flight engineer's stations being shoulder to shoulder, as it were. Again, Cotterell second-guessed my objection.

'Later, switching to heavy bombers, after we'd picked up our mid-upper gunner and flight engineer, we still did the same.' He gave a short laugh. 'Not so easily then, especially with the Lanc's compass being situated where it was, but it had become a sort of talisman. Our lucky charm if you like. Our "chummy huddle" our eng called it. So I'd squeeze in, set the compass, then hover there, looking out at the flak and fireworks, until the turn was completed. Then I'd call 'On heading, Skip,' and scuttle back to my cubicle and its curtain.

His tone, which had become animated, sobered.

'I know that's the procedure he would have used then, too. For he had his hands fuller that day than he could ever have envisaged. Needed every bit of luck.'

His voice died away. But I waited. Until eventually he resumed, heavily, 'If I could only be certain, I swear I'd die happy. And, you know –' he was barely murmuring now, 'I really believe they would finally – get their peace ... so well deserved ...'

Uncomfortable as this made me feel, and for some time now I had begun getting increasingly uncomfortable, I became suddenly and reluctantly aware that there was at least one other dimension operating here. For in that moment it came to me that this was not, as I had first thought, simply a lamentation for the injustice he believed to have been done to his own crew.

Certainly it came from Cotterell, and concerned his own crew. But beyond that it was, in microcosm, a plea against injustice from all those in Bomber Command whose wartime contribution has been so disgracefully disparaged; lions all, yet so often portrayed these days as donkeys burdened with moral disrepute. Although burdened, in fairness, not just by rose-spectacled after-the-event do-gooders, but also by contemporaries honestly driven by higher-sphere humanitarian considerations. Heroes notwithstanding, engaged on winning a war they regarded as being fought against injustice.

I merely grunted, however, absently nodding my acquiescence down the phone. For although I followed with increasing reluctance, professionalism still pointed me towards that so-fraught inbound turn over the sea. Insisting that I visualise a relatively inexperienced pilot with very serious control problems setting his own compass before a reversal of direction. At night. And in thick cloud. His only aid to keeping control of his aircraft the limited number of flight instruments the loss of his artificial horizon had left him.

As it came time to turn he would take his eyes off actually controlling the crippled machine, bend down, peer at the dimly-lit compass, unlock the grid ring, rotate it until – But enough!

For by then, even without a windmilling propeller, he would be lucky if the aircraft had merely rolled into a steep bank. Let alone fallen into a spiral dive. Or a spin – in those circumstances almost certainly unrecoverable. And this before even commencing the turn!

No, infinitely better to let the presently-unoccupied navigator come forward and set the compass for you. And better still, have him remain there while you sat for what might be as little as three minutes, but what would seem an interminable time, oh-so-gently! nursing the tottering aircraft around the turn. All the while the nav could monitor the compass, allowing you to concentrate on scanning the flight-attitude instruments and maintaining control, knowing that the moment it was time to stop the turn he would tell you. It was crew co-operation of the highest order.

But spiralling out of control in the turn had to be the way of it! Common sense and my working store of airmanship insisted upon it being so, notwithstanding my ever increasing, and still quite inexplicable, reluctance to hold to this view. Yet Cotterell was convinced that the turn had not been the problem; had obsessively held to that for far longer than I had been flying. Just for the sake of argument, then ...

'So if Norris was thinking west instead of east ... And inadvertently set the wrong one ...'

'No, that still wouldn't gel ...'

Nor would it. For the pilot would, by rote, have been taking in the compass, albeit sketchily enough, as part of his scan.

In my mind's eye I could almost see the unhappy young navigator, unsure of himself, the odd one out in a crew who were by this time, on their final operation of the tour, more nearly kin to one another than the members of many a provenly-devoted family. That he would have been flustered, and that he might make the same basic error he had made in pilot training, but this time with fatal consequences, was only too conceivable.

Yet again I had to ask myself what this was all about. For even if that had indeed been the case, who was to say? Certainly not Cotterell. For regardless of Jack Norris's error in training, there could be never be any proof that he had sent his crew the wrong way on that baleful night. Not this long after the event. No overturning, therefore, even morally, the verdict of the court of inquiry which had blamed the loss on the pilot's failure to maintain control when over the sea. And blame pilot; blame entire crew. All hapless six of them; each demonstrably competent in his own role, each powerless to have assisted his pilot. But guilty as found. Which was the way of the world.

Cotterell might not like it. Yet crap happens! And damningly unfair as a false finding was to the memory of both the pilot and his crew, nothing on earth could resolve the matter now.

Only suddenly, disconcertingly, the last bastion of my pragmatism came under threat. For the maggot in my brain was wriggling free at last. Nothing about sheep! Nothing about shepherding lore! What came to the surface instead was a snippet from a supposedly-forgotten conversation with a ex-wartime navigator, many years before!

'I upset him, too – Jack,' I blurted down the line, a little breathlessly, for all my endeavour to retain control. 'The other chap had clearly been needling him, and I asked what he'd said. It had struck a cord, so I probably put two and two together and made five.' Despite the increasing turmoil in my mind I couched my next words designedly, not wishing to cue him. 'All I caught was something about red.'

I heard a catch of breath at the far end of the line; but I was carried away by the light still breaking over me. And by the appalling realisation that if what, for a fortnight or more before that fateful day, I had believed to be merely a subliminal niggle proved instead to be some form of precognition; that if what I had held to be a serendipitous encounter on Kinder was now revealed as nothing of the sort, but a meeting that had, in fact, been predestined regardless of the dictates of time and space, indeed of life and death themselves, then the implications were immense. Unspeakable even. Yet, what hope they might offer! A power that simply could not be! A power that held in its gift deliverance from guilt! And yet –, surely unthinkable, at best.

'Tell me –' Cotterell's exhortation came through as a gasp.

'I asked if what he'd called out was "Red on –"'

'Blue!' Cotterell's interjection exploded in my ear. 'I knew it. I just bloody knew it! All these years I've been only too bloody right!' He was shouting at the top of his voice. But there was no exultation in his tone, no satisfaction at having been proven correct, only passion, passion grown virulent during sixty years of suppression. His outburst cut off abruptly. And this time he did not even put a palm over the mouthpiece. 'It's all right, my dear,' his voice was appreciably lower, 'I'll tell you all about it in a while.'

When he addressed himself to me again, his voice was not only lower, but back under control. Almost schoolmasterish. For my part I now knew exactly what he was going to tell me. Or the gist of it. But it was not for me to forestall him. Not after all his obsessive years.

'In detail, here's the way Skip worked it. I'd set the required heading, say, west. Then he'd roll into the turn, keeping his eyes on the attitude instruments. Meanwhile, I'd watch the compass, and when, eventually, I saw the pointer – the red end of the needle – come sailing around to meet the red north mark, I'd call, "West, Skip". At which Skip would stop the turn. And that was wizard, we were pointing in the right direction: "Red on Red, safe to bed!" that was the by-word.'

He stopped. Snorted. A very hasty snort. Then resumed. Only as he continued his emotion increasingly threatened to break through his now-brittle reserve.

'By convention the tail end of the needle – in reality the compass-card pointer, as you'll know, – was always known as the blue end. If you got careless, and stopped the turn when the tail end of the needle sailed around to the red north mark, then it was curtains. "Red on Blue: this you'll rue!"'

He coughed. 'Set Red on Blue and you were pointing in the reciprocal direction: west instead of east; Berlin instead of bloody Britain; QDR instead of QDM; go instead of come; twelve o'clock instead of six o'clock. It's what the bastard did in training. And it's what the bastard did that night.' Cotterell's voice, which had been gaining in stridency throughout, suddenly and distressingly broke.

'I don't know what, but something about you has given them what I believe they've been searching for, the opportunity to earn them their peace. At least – thanks to you – they'll rest now.'

He choked back what was clearly a sob. 'I'm sorry. You'll have to get back to me,' he gulped, 'another time.'

As in a vignette the scene appeared before me. The dark night, thick with cloud, full rudder, and wheel hard over as far as it would go, just to hold the crippled machine on the course the navigator had set, towards the sea. Then easing into the inbound turn to port, all control forces changing, the machine sluggish, juddering on the extreme limit of control. The pilot's eyes glued to the turn and slip, for incessant throat-parching minutes on end. The so-eagerly awaited advisory from the navigator – from young Jack –, hovering over the compass.

'West! – on heading, Skip!' and rolling, egg-gentle, out of the turn towards the field.

The turn successfully completed! Against all the odds. Safely inbound to base at 2,000 feet, gingerly settling and re-trimming the aircraft, left leg stiff, both hands fully occupied. Then preparing to ease into the descent, to begin feeling downwards, secure in the knowledge that the cloud will part as the altimeter reads eight hundred feet, the hours, the weeks, the months, of unremitting nervous tension, now, at tour's end, behind them for a finite space of time. With the strong wind speeding them over the surface they must have re-crossed the coast some time since, but even the Wolds would be a good 1,600 feet below.

'OK, Eng, you do the throttles.'

And the flight engineer acquiescing, ready and unsurprised at the role change in this extremity, his gauntleted hands closing on the levers, and firming, to smoothly ease off the power. And then, on the instant! – the sudden, quite inexplicable touch beneath the belly! Where there should be nothing to touch for over forty miles! The frantic craning. Ahead at the altimeter – a safe 2,000 feet plus! Then eyes, suddenly wild with alarm, dropping to the dimly-lit compass, seeing west, set exactly as it should be. Then assimilating that Red is not on Red, but on Blue! And comprehending, as at a second touch the world explodes in a welter of fire, rushes, petrol, and peat-black water.

The line had gone dead. And I knew that I, for my part, would never dial that number again. Shaken to the core, I let the phone settle onto its rest, and looked blankly at the shelved far wall of the flat, at the books, and at the festive cards ...

So Helen had been right. There had, after all, been a gift-giving power to rid me of my demons. It was gratifying, of course, that the fellow flyers who had delivered me had thereby secured their own deliverance. For that my sense of guilt had been deemed fair exchange for their sense of injustice I could have no doubt. Yet there was no elation, only awe, at the revelation that the co-dependency had been predestined. In an act of utter abnegation I pushed aside my port. I had neither the taste for it, nor the need for its support.

But God, how I needed Helen's!

Glossary

'Ack-Ack', p115: British anti-aircraft batteries.

The Rime of the Ancient Mariner (1798), p91: Samuel Taylor Coleridge (1772-1834).

Clough, p8: a moorland valley, or ravine.

Sir Arthur Conan Doyle (1859-1930), p56: the fictional Great Grimpen Mire in his *Hound of the Baskervilles* is a bog in which sphagnum moss floats above trapped ground water.

Darcey Andrea Bussell (b.1969), p81: principal ballerina with the Royal Ballet

Derbyshire Gritstone, p13: a black-and-white-faced, hornless sheep.

Dowson, p48: Ernest Dowson (1867-1900), from whose poem *Non Sum Aqualis Eram*, Margaret Mitchell took the title for her 1936 '*Gone with the Wind*'.

Geopathic stress, p32: a fringe theory which holds that benign rays are constantly rising through the earth but turn harmful when they are impeded.

Sir William Schwenck Gilbert (1836-1911), p57: librettist, *The Pirates of Penzance.*

Grough, p26: a gully or channel eroded by water in upland peat moors.

Gyros, p72: the spinning mass of a gyroscope makes changing its direction difficult, gyros therefore, are commonly used in instruments which are required to maintain their equilibrium.

Hag (alternative, hagg), p26: a relatively high and firm place in a bog. The rough, overhanging edge of a peat hole.

Height, p16: the vertical distance above the surface. (Altitude is the vertical distance above mean sea level)

Kinder Mass Trespass, p17: romantic, and largely derivative, accounts abound. For those wishing make their own assessment of this 1932 foray, contemporary sources are readily available.

Lady Bracknell, p106: in Oscar Wilde's, *The Importance of Being Earnest,* of 1895.

Ley lines, p32: straight lines between landscape features. Thought by some to have scientific or magical significance.

Lewis Carroll, p22: *Through The Looking-Glass And What Alice Found There* (1871). Charles Lutwidge Dodgson (1832-1898)

Magnetic North Pole, p32: essentially, the location to which a compass needle points, as opposed to the Geographic North Pole, which is the axis of the earth's rotation.

Oscar Wilde (1854-1900), p29: see also Lady Bracknell, above.

Operational Training Unit (OTU), p113: a typical transition was from the twin-engined Wellington to the four-engined Halifax or Stirling; then to the Lancaster.

Pigpen, p76: a dirt-attracting character in *Peanuts* by Charles M. Schultz (1922-2000)

QDR for QDM, p126: in a brevity code designed for use in morse-code communications QDM was a course to reach a station, QDR a bearing from that station. For an aircraft north of a station the course to steer (QDM) would be south, its bearing from the station (QDR) north.

Red on Red; Red on Blue, p126: linked mnemonics. In magnetic theory, and in the RAF's 1941 *Air Navigation* manual (p183 et seq) the north-seeking needle was red, its tail end blue. Even though the aircraft compass had a card rather than a needle, and a normally black 'tail', the *Red on Blue* aide-memoire lived on: not least in the (surely?) apocryphal story, 'They set red on blue and so bombed Dublin instead of Dortmund'. An alternative was 'red on black'

Serendipity, p72: Horace Walpole (1717-1797) coined the word to the sense of what he termed, 'the silly fairy tale', *The Three Princes of Serendip*, 1754.

Snake Path, p17: agreement for this public way from Hayfield to The Snake Inn was achieved in 1897. The route was initially marked by white poles and 'no divergence or trespass ' notices.

'terribly unforgiving …', p16: from a 1931 paper to The Royal Aeronautical Society by Captain A.G. Lamplugh, Deputy Master of the Guild of Air Pilots and Air Navigators (1935-1936).

Tolkienesque, p75: John Ronald Reuel Tolkien, CBE (1892-1973), *The Hobbit* (1937

Turn and slip (to wartime pilots, 'turn and bank'), p127: a 'needle and ball' instrument which indicates the rate at which the machine is turning, and whether that turn is properly balanced.

Acknowledgements

The author would like to express his appreciation to all those who proofread this story – originally written for Wies' 2001 Christmas present. Particular thanks go to Frances Meeks, Ethna and Geoff Clarke, Clive Teale, Ian Howe, Margaret Poulson, Marian Draper, Myfanwy James, Jane Foster, Dave Allsup, Mike Brown, Fred James DFC, Stella Porter, and Ken Johnson. But above all to Wies, who from the start militated against 'all that walking and all those aeroplanes'.

ISBN 978-0-9556325-0-1